Burnt Out

Burnt Out

CLARE CURZON

First published in Great Britain in 2009 by
Allison & Busby Limited
13 Charlotte Mews
London W1T 4EJ
www.allisonandbusby.com

A CIP catalogue record for this book is available from
the British Library.

10 9 8 7 6 5 4 3 2 1

13-ISBN 978-0-7490-0711-9

Typeset in 13.5/16.5 pt Adobe Garamond Pro by
Allison & Busby Ltd

The paper used for this Allison & Busby publication
has been produced from trees that have been legally sourced
from well-managed and credibly certified forests.

PEFC
PEFC/16-33-111
CATG-PEFC-052
www.pefc.org

Printed and bound in Great Britain by
MPG Books Ltd, Bodmin, Cornwall

CLARE CURZON began writing in the 1960s and has published over forty novels under a variety of pseudonyms. She studied French and Psychology at King's College, London, and much of her work is concerned with the dynamics within closely knit communities. A grandmother to seven, in her free time she enjoys travel and painting. Clare lives in Buckinghamshire.

Available from
ALLISON **& B**USBY

In the Mike Yeadings series
Body of a Woman
A Meeting of Minds
Last to Leave
The Glass Wall
The Edge
Payback
Off Track
Burnt Out

Prologue

Early morning, Sunday, 23rd November

It seemed like just another car crashed and torched overnight in the wooded area between Fulmer and Stoke Poges. A passing motorist reported the smoking wreck and a fire tender was despatched at 3.12 a.m. to get it sorted and confirm that it was fully burnt out.

In summer the surrounding heathland was vulnerable. Fires would spread fast, consuming the silver birches. They would seem to be extinguished, and then burst out again under the peaty surface. But after a drenching autumn, and now early frosts, this was a routine shout.

Thames Valley's Traffic Division was notified and a police patrol car sent out from Amersham station. Nothing new, the uniformed driver assumed. It would be the familiar story of lively lads nicking what had been a rather snazzy number for a weekend's speed-racing. The winning vehicle would have taken the revellers on after some spectacular fireworks.

Kids round here were sophisticated, drove almost as soon

as they could toddle, and had enough experience not to leave clues. There might, or might not, be something to pick up from the tyre tracks of a second car, but that wasn't his worry. Scenes of Crime Officers would be checking it all over in daylight, if Traffic Div considered referring it to CID.

For him, tomorrow's job would be spent warmly indoors, checking the Audi's ownership and phoning round the news. The sorry owner, whoever they are, would need to arrange disposal and be given an accident report number to put in an insurance claim. Not his concern. Only another hour on duty and he could return to the nick.

There was quite a bit of hanging around until the fire team decided the wreck was cool enough to work on, and then they did the routine busting open to see what was inside.

That was when things started livening up, because when they reached the boot and sprung the lock they found it wasn't empty.

It went suddenly quiet. The firemen had clustered to peer in. PC Tom Withers abandoned the peppermint-scented fug of the control car to stroll across and join them. With five and a half years of traffic duty under his belt, he had dealt with bodies of all varieties, but nothing like this.

It was blackened and shrivelled like one of those embalmed Ancient Egyptians after a couple of millennia in their tomb. But the horror was in the writhing shape, the contorted, screaming face. He stared, unable to look away, knowing he'd see it in nightmares for the rest of his life.

* * *

10

The call came through to DCI Angus Mott at 5.19 a.m. on Sunday morning and, still half asleep, he threshed about to find the phone. The far side of the bed was empty. Paula must have gone to quieten the crying baby, and he'd slept right through it. 'Sir,' he growled, recognising the Boss's voice, 'Wassup?'

It seemed that a severely charred body had been discovered in a burnt-out Audi Cabriolet, crashed in a country lane between Fulmer and Stoke Poges. Not in the driver's seat, but the boot.

He'd have to get out there and check that uniform had properly secured the crime scene before their size eleven boots eliminated any clues the fire crew had left.

He swung out of bed, conscious that a pathetic wailing had started up elsewhere in the apartment. As he threw clothes on, Paula came in rocking the baby in her arms.

'I'd just got her off and the damn phone woke her again,' she complained.

'She's not the only protester. I didn't get back from the GBH until almost two. Salmon and Silver are on a surveillance for a drugs drop and Z's away. There's only Beaumont and me. God, what I'd give for just one phone-free, silent-baby night.'

It's cruel to be still calling their new arrival 'the baby', he thought as he drove off. It was more than time to settle on a name. But what? Paula had suggested some feminine form of Attila would suit the squalling infant.

Just colic, the visiting nurse had assured them. Last week she'd promised it would settle itself in the end. That end seemed a long time coming.

* * *

11

The verge where Angus parked had thawed out, but grass farther from the fire and foam was still stiffly white with overnight frost. There was already a police presence at the crime scene. Two cars, blue lights flashing, were closer to the wreck than he cared for, but in one the occupants had sense enough to stay inside. Two other uniformed officers were securing the crime scene with bollards and plastic tape.

Behind him a white van pulled up; a collapsible tent and more traffic cones were unloaded. Angus got out and went back to check on operations.

'Hold back until SOCO's had a first look. The emergency services will have trampled over everything, but there might be something left for their cameras to pick up.'

'Looks a pretty thorough job; must have lit up the neighbourhood like a beacon.'

Angus agreed silently: quite a Saturday night party piece. From here, the rear number plate seemed melted, the figures lost. He walked along the grass verge, passing the two police cars, and scanned the front of the wreck. Headlights, bumper and valance were buckled where the car had been driven into a tree several yards into the woodland. The bonnet was crushed like an empty beer can.

There was no licence plate. In view of the concealed body, was it removed deliberately to delay identification? Could this torching be not the work of mindless yobbos but the owner's doing, a desperate attempt to gain time while he contrived an alibi or disappeared into thin air?

In which case, the murder was premeditated, and not only vicious but a tad more sophisticated than he'd been expecting. Traffic Division could expect to receive a stolen car report for this make of car in the next few hours, either genuine or as cover-up.

He watched Beaumont's red Toyota join the string of cars by the verge. He walked back as the DS got out. 'I want the front licence plate recovered as soon as there's a taped route through,' he ordered.

Beaumont nodded, taking in the blackened state of the wreck. There was considerable distortion of the bodywork, the retractable roof had entirely burnt away and the boot now yawned open. That would have been the fire crew's work. Heat wouldn't have sprung it that far.

Mott left him to it, walking back to his car. The Boss would need details as soon as it was light. But why wait? After he'd passed Mott the initial message, Superintendent Yeadings would have abandoned bed and gone to make strong coffee. It was already 6.27 a.m.

His phone call from the car was picked up by Yeadings' young daughter.

'Daddy's busy.'

'I know, Sally. It's breakfast time. But just ask him to ring Angus on his mobile, would you?'

'I know it's you, Angus. I recognised your voice. But he's still busy.'

'Just give him my—'

'Hello?' This was Nan overriding the obstruction. 'Can I help you?'

'I'm with the body Mike notified, Nan. Country

lane between Fulmer and Stoke Poges. It could turn out interesting. I thought Mike should know.'

'Angus, I'm sorry: that was Sally being protective. I'll get Mike right away. He's just finished his meal.'

'Angus, should I come?' Yeadings asked as he took over the phone.

'There's not much call at the moment.' He described the scene. 'We're waiting for the full SOCO team.'

'Get Beaumont in, or Z.'

'Z's away this weekend, left yesterday,' Angus reminded him. 'Christmas shopping in France with Max. Beaumont's already here.'

'Right. Well, I'll be in early, 0800 hours sharp. Thanks for the warning, Angus.'

Over the line DI Salmon sounded his usual morose self. The night's vigil hadn't turned up any activity at the lock-up garages he and Silver had been watching. He'd be tired, but Angus guessed he wasn't actually averse to escaping a domestic Sabbath. Beaumont, when rung earlier, had sworn. He'd intended spending the afternoon painting the garden furniture ready for over-winter storage.

'They're threatening rain once the frost lets up, and I have to finish this outdoors.'

'Z's away,' Angus had reminded him and waited for the significance to sink in. Beaumont was never slow to steal a march on Rosemary Zyczynski. Both qualified for promotion to inspector; they had long been competing for the next vacancy. Beaumont considered that Z had an unfair advantage, being a woman. Not that it made her in any way superior; just a better fit for the politically correct statistics. 'Thirty minutes,' he'd promised Angus, and was there in just over twenty-seven.

By now the full SOCO team was assembled at the crash scene in their white overalls and starting their minute inspection of the wreck, shining torches in, scraping up samples, fanning out to inspect the surrounding area. The young medic on call turned up, confirmed death, and stood about shivering with his hands in his pockets.

'It hardly needed a professional opinion,' he complained, viewing the incinerated body folded in the car boot. 'No way is it going to walk away from this. Where will you take it?'

'Wexham Park morgue, unless the Prof has a preference.' *It*, Angus noted, was how the doctor had referred to the body. 'Any idea of gender?' he asked.

'Not the way it is right now, and not my concern in any case. I've done my bit. You have a corpse, and that's official. No need to hang around, is there?'

He mooched off, retrieved his classic sports car from the verge and roared away, flinging up turf and gravel.

The technicians were still busy measuring and taking photographs. Any tyre tracks from last evening had been made when the road was damp from sleet. Later, frost had hardened the surface, but now the traces were thawing and fragile. It wouldn't be easy fixing a time to each stage. Already police and fire service vehicles had produced a network of over-tracking on the road.

Lab work, processing and enhancing of photographs, was a fiddly business but it had the advantage of being indoors. This was no day to be freezing on your feet out here and idly speculating on the crime. Beaumont was missing the relative activity of painting garden chairs.

DCI Angus Mott felt obliged to stay on to see the body bagged and transferred to an unmarked van, then decided to knock off, leaving Salmon in charge. '8 a.m. with your reports,' he told the other two CID men. 'The Boss is coming in. You'll just about make it.'

'Sunday,' Beaumont said grimly, as though he had something personal against the day. DI Salmon rocked on his heels, looking as near satisfied as his features ever showed.

There was little as yet for the morning's briefing, but they had at least established one piece of information about the new case. The body, initially checked over at the morgue before Prof Littlejohn's full post-mortem, was considered to be that of a woman aged between twenty-five and forty-five.

Chapter One

Friday, 14th November

Orange and scarlet flames were writhing from the ground-floor windows, heavy black smoke almost obscuring the three children screaming at the upper floor. Women in the little group massed beyond the garden gate were yelling up to them, 'Jump! Come on, you kids. For God's sake, jump!'

Below, thick cushions hastily piled on a sofa wobbled as helpers struggled to make a safe landing for them. In striped pyjamas and dressing gown, a neighbour was directing his garden hose towards the flames, but the feeble stream of water struck the blackened brickwork and instantly turned to steam.

Monotonously, out in the road, a runaway dog kept up a frenzied barking.

'Where the hell's the fire service?' came a near-demented cry.

As though on cue, a distant siren was heard, amplified over a matter of seconds, and then the fire engine roared round the corner by the newsagent's, greeted with a ragged cheer. The little crowd scattered as the machine drew up close in the road. Firefighters started leaping out, two still struggling into their uniform trousers. One ran to the hoses and began unreeling while another connected hoses to pump.

Four, three, two, one, and the full force of 7 bar of water burst forth, knocking the first man off his feet. Uncontrolled, the hose leapt like a live creature. Water jetted over the crowd, who shrieked, falling back against the fence.

'Cut,' cried an amplified voice. 'That's great, boys!'

'Like hell it is!' A second, sharper voice cut through as the female director rose from her bank of monitors. 'No! The whole take's rubbished. A woman in front of the crowd cowered before the water struck. Yes, you in the blue plastic curlers: just get lost. I want the set dried out, then the whole take repeated. And get a move on. You know how delays increase costs.'

The girl with the megaphone shrivelled visibly. 'Can't we work this over in the edit? A second camera had another angle on it.' Her words trailed away, faced by the indomitable Margot's scowl.

The props team's mumble of rebellion was kept low, covered in part by the necessary clatter of restoring the scene and bringing in propane heaters.

'Or could you fake rainfall to cover it?' asked the actor in the station officer's white helmet, but the suggestion was overridden.

'Roger, you can't suddenly script rain in. Logically, it

would keep the crowd away,' the director bit back, 'and extras are on a fixed budget. Keep to your job and I'll keep to mine.'

Her mouth was a single tight line. Why the hell had she been persuaded to take on this farcical package, a firefighters' version of the *Keystone Cops* with minimal heroics and abysmal dialogue? They'd said it would be as popular as *Dad's Army*, but audiences had moved on since those war-obsessed days. She'd set her heart on getting the third series of *Craven Court*, but the head of light entertainment hadn't seen eye to eye with her over that, and nothing equally substantive had been in the offing.

She was wasted on outdated humour like this. After the last rushes were shown even the producer, Greg Victor, had grunted, hummed, and remarked that comedy was something you either 'could do' or you couldn't; then gone off to the bar to sulk. That didn't promise any BAFTA awards for the series.

Her eyes swung to the health and safety officer, approaching with clipboard at the ready. He'd start niggling over the fire hazards again. Charm never worked with him and, the way she felt right now, she could only bare her teeth in anger. Margot's chin jutted as she prepared to fight her corner.

Her assistant director ran a hand through her cropped copper hair. It had been a long day. At this rate they'd never finish on time tonight. Jenny Barnes watched Margot in despair. The damn woman had eyes like a hawk for the action: never missed the most minor flaw. Because of it, the already depleted crowd scene had lost another body.

The stunt actor had barely flinched and it could easily have been edited out. Two other cameras had been working on the crowd scene.

Margot's stance was changing from stiff-shouldered, hand-on-hip and weight-on-one-leg, to a slight easing of posture. Now she was resting a hand on Health and Safety's arm and leading him off towards the caravan for an Irish coffee.

To follow her boss was tempting, but Jenny needed a break from her. She walked back to the car park, where she found Jamie's old Nissan unlocked and with its key still in the ignition. She climbed in, switched on the engine and turned up the heating. She guessed the outer temperature could be only a couple of degrees above freezing.

Across at the fire scene, the gas jets had been extinguished and the props team were scurrying about under arc lamps, checking on the damage. The mock-up frontage of the house stood dark and silent, the child actors having been led down the rear steps and taken away for a supplementary snack.

Jenny groped under the dashboard and retrieved her half-empty Thermos of tomato soup. There were things she should be checking on instead of cowering here, but sometimes it was better to go missing than have Margot catch her working on something she'd condemn out of hand. Assistant director sounded good when she'd made the grade, but there were aspects she hadn't reckoned on: mainly her boss. Margot would sit hooked to the monitors, while her own job was to scuttle about checking the whole damn shoot on scene.

Not that Margot wasn't sharp. In some ways she was someone you could learn from, but clearly this time she had issues with the series. She'd brought a barely disguised attitude of contempt to the script, and as work progressed she treated any modifications Jenny suggested with equal scorn. It was intensely frustrating, because this sort of light comedy was really up her street. She knew if she was given a free rein she could spur the cast on to greater enthusiasm. All they needed at this point was encouragement. Get the lighting team laughing: that was the key. Slapstick farce might bore the pants off them, but they weren't deaf to a witty line of dialogue. And this script had some real winners, if delivered with the right timing.

Four hours later Margot was ready to leave. She begrudged the fifteen minutes wasted in the canteen caravan with the producer, Greg Victor, enduring his lukewarm commentary on the shoot. It was interrupted halfway by a phone call for her from Oliver, offering to pick her up from the location at Fulham. He was heading for home from Soho.

She didn't need his offer and said so quite specifically, but she doubted he got the message due to the groundswell of shouted conversation in the background. With luck, she'd be gone before he arrived.

But as she made it to the main street a car pulled up alongside. There were four men inside, rowdy and half drunk.

She'd no intention of joining them. Even with Toby Frobisher at the wheel, it was too risky. 'Badger' Gibbons, crushed in the rear seat between Oliver and some other

21

body they'd have picked up at Ronnie Scott's, was making funky noises on his trumpet, punctuated by raucous farting.

'Go to hell,' she told her husband, and stuck out a hand for her ordered taxi. It pulled forward smartly and she ran the few yards to catch up. 'Marylebone,' she shouted to the driver.

'Railway station?' he demanded moodily.

Of course the railway station. Did he think she wanted the bloody police station? Well, maybe, in view of the company she had just refused. She clamped her mouth shut, withering him with a glance.

She was barely in time for the last train. Settled in a corner, she closed her eyes, wiping out the other passengers: half a dozen bevvied-up kids giggling over a shared vodka bottle, their antics scrupulously ignored by middle-aged, immaculately coiffed couples returning from London theatres or hotel dinners; doubtless also the odd businessman who'd tell the wife he'd 'needed to work late'.

Soothed by the monotonous drumming of wheels on rails, she did sleep for a few minutes. When she awoke they were passing through one of those dark spaces between stations. Mentally she was still with the TV show she'd been filming and the half-burnt-out location they'd found in Fulham.

As the train slowed, passengers began collecting their possessions. Some stood and started edging towards the doors. Lights slid across outside, but the station's name was obscured. She saw it wasn't her own: somewhere in the countryside.

Instantly, as the double doors began to close again, she was on her feet, lurching towards them. She punched the release button and fell through into the chill night air. On an alien platform.

It was weird: an inexplicable compulsion not to be left in there alone.

The straggling crowd moved on ahead, breaking up to file through an open archway, dropping their tickets on the ground or shoving them with gloved hands into bulky coat pockets.

Station staff had gone off duty and only a single dim lamp hung at the exit; not a taxi to be had.

The voices were dispersing, becoming distant, high-pitched against the cold, then came the unsynchronised slamming of doors in the car park. And then she was left in silence. But where? She had no idea.

Where and *unaware*. She felt a little mad, standing there grinning over the rhyming words as the sleet began, beading her uncovered hair. Her coat was snug, but she'd left her pashmina beside her seat in the train.

She walked out into the village street, and saw it was one she'd occasionally driven through: Little Chalfont. Vaguely that disappointed her, being almost familiar when she'd expected to plunge rashly into the unknown.

She'd felt the sudden need for risk – when risk was what she'd already turned down, refusing the lift with her husband's drunken friends. She wasn't totally sober herself, although she'd guarded her glass and waved away a few refills, already on a minor high at the final sorting of the evening, and with the news that the next two episodes of *All Fired Up* were now agreed. It seemed the people in charge didn't share her low opinion of the script. At least it meant continuity of work, being still there among the 'in' crowd.

And, leaving the half-hearted congratulations behind, without previous intention she'd achieved a public act of severance: at last making a stand against Oliver, showing she didn't need him. Not for a lift home. Not for anything. He'd become excess baggage.

'Go to hell,' she'd told him, meaning it, although normally she was sparing with swear words. But tonight nothing was quite normal, and perversely she liked it that way.

She scrabbled in her bag for her mobile phone, dialled her home number, and overrode Joanna's objections, insisting she stay on till morning. There were always a couple of beds left made up for incapable dinner guests or for when the child-minder needed to sleep overnight.

Joanna argued, of course, but agreed at the promise of an extra thirty pounds.

Ahead, the little parade of closed shops was silent. Sodium street lamps, reflected on the sleekly wet road, looked like barley-sugar twists. The spaces between them seemed to increase beyond the turn to Nightingale Lane, leaving black holes to be filled up with ambiguous half shadows.

She turned right, believing that if she continued walking eventually there'd be two pubs, one on each side of the road. Surely in one of them someone would still be up, clearing tables and stacking chairs ready for the morning cleaners.

Even if they didn't take overnighters, maybe she could get a room there. Tonight anything was better than going home.

The bed felt lumpy; the pillows were of the solid, rubbery kind that heated up as soon as you laid your head down. The pub wasn't accustomed to putting up guests and she'd had to pay over the odds to persuade them. Lone women at night, without luggage, were a risk in themselves, it seemed.

Margot lay awake trying to account for how she had arrived at this relative discomfort, not at all sure that it had been from her own choice. But if not, who or what could she blame this sudden whim on? A general discontent with the way she'd allowed her life to become so channelled?

But with what specifically? Her marriage, certainly. For a long time she'd known it had failed. Also being a leading director, but being given a substandard show to cobble together? Somehow losing vital rapport with her team on the set? All of that, but there was something more, something new that went deeper, making her feel an unusual sensation of missing out.

This morning she'd been full of pizzazz, confident she could tackle anything the day threw at her and come through shining. So, since then, what had happened – or failed to happen – to make the difference? At what point had this other mood taken her over?

Since sleep seemed out of the question, she should try to sort it out now, going through every choice she'd made, every move, every hiccup in the production. She heaved herself up on her elbows, staring into the dark, and ran the day, like film rushes, through again.

It had happened right at the start, with Greg Victor's vandalism of the day's script. All right, it needed something done, but his proposed changes didn't guarantee improvement. They'd all done what they could to patch the new stuff in, but instead of a sense of achievement over that, she'd felt let down.

The sense of losing had been inevitable, like a helium balloon slowly deflating. Not a pinprick so that the thing exploded, but with a slack knotting at base so that gradually the gas escaped, almost unnoticeably at first. And then came the shrivelling, the flabbiness, her creeping loss of control.

She'd taken it out on the wrong people. Maybe the techs hadn't been as clumsy as she'd thought at the time. But old Walter, his mind already set on retirement, was so stuck-in-the-mud. She'd chewed him up because, as senior cameraman, he wasn't ready to accept new ideas, take chances. Not that the blame for risks taken would ever be laid at his door.

At the additional planning meeting inserted between takes that afternoon he'd been called away to his retirement seminar. In his absence, Number Two Camera had voiced doubts about the shoot's lagging tempo. He'd suggested inserting a brief scene, to bring in the upstairs bedroom where the kids were panicking. It would give a chance to work on some exciting close-ups; plenty of choking smoke and blurred images: a new dimension and added drama.

With little more than two adjacent walls and some

planked flooring, there wasn't room up there to take in the usual equipment, so to save the fee for hiring a crane – possibly somewhere in the region of £10,000 – he could bring in a lightweight camera and shoot shoulder-high from a ladder behind the façade.

But when she'd put it to Walter on his return he'd turned it down flat. He was Number One Camera; the script said external shooting, and he intended it to stay that way.

Then Nicco, on camera two, had offered to fix it himself. No sweat: he was OK with ladders, could climb like a monkey.

It was inspired; she was all for it. But she hadn't missed the other's reaction. In the ensuing silence, Walter, faced by her approval of the offer, had stared long and hard at the young man, incredulous that now, on his final series, he could be challenged, dethroned even before he was out of the door.

But her decision had been right, even if poor protocol. It was a smart idea, and Walter had finally had to give in, because there wasn't a place for him in it.

Tomorrow she must somehow make up for his humiliation, but without weakly reinstating things the way they'd been. She couldn't risk losing authority in front of everyone, and anyway, the young man must have been next in line to take the senior job once Walter left. That was outside her remit.

She lay back, enjoying the little shiver of chill as she burrowed again under the unheated covers. Now, perhaps, she would sleep. Closing her eyes, she saw an image of the young cameraman's eager face, the dark eyes, black curls tumbling over his broad forehead, the brilliance of a wide, white smile. Quick-moving, motivated, handsome; maybe ethnic Greek or Italian. Everyone called him Nicco. She must find out more about him, encourage his enthusiasm.

She wondered why he'd become a cameraman. With drama school training, he'd have been the ideal romantic lead. She could see him in the title role of a re-make of *The Charmer* or in costume drama as another Darcy; even a reckless Musketeer riding bareback through a forest of ancient oaks, his scarlet cloak streaming in the wind...

Mesmerised by the imagined thudding of hooves, her eyelids grew heavy. She was sliding into sleep. And the swashbuckling figure rode wildly on ahead.

Jenny Barnes had sat waiting, huddled in the old brown Nissan, until Jamie finished clearing the scene. As floor manager, he was usually the last to leave. He came back whistling, laptop tucked under one arm and two styrofoam beakers of coffee in his hands. She leant across to open the driver's door as he stood there.

'Mind yourself, it's bloody scalding. Which is more than I'd say for the weather.'

Incorrigibly cheerful as ever, which infuriated her when she needed a listener to empathise with her present complaints. Nevertheless she tried for it, and he came back with a consolatory, 'Poor old girl. Still, you must admit our Margot is right there on the ball.'

Our Margot! She could throttle him. Why must he include her in his one-man fan club? Couldn't he see that

Margot sat solidly on her chances of promotion?

They continued to drink their coffee in silence, warming their hands round the beakers until finally he tossed his, empty, over his shoulder to join the collected debris in the car's rear. 'OK then, gorgeous; your place or mine?'

Jenny sighed. Did it matter? Whichever, he wasn't the Romeo she needed right now. If only he'd gone for English Literature instead of Stagecraft she could warm to his approach more readily. As it was, this must be another price to pay for a lift back to Notting Hill. And by Monday she'd have her own transport, a powerful Kawasaki Ninja. No further need for Jamie then.

'Mine,' she said firmly, and realised she'd sounded just like Margot.

Chapter Two

'Idiot!' Margot said aloud on waking. She remembered her previous night's eccentricity and sat bolt upright in bed.

But it's Saturday, she consoled herself. Whatever mistakes she'd made yesterday belonged to the past working week. Saturday and Sunday were the blank-out days before she had to wrestle again with schedules, actors' tantrums and an inadequate script.

But then weekends weren't all that smart either. She'd have to get home now to Great Missenden, pay Joanna off; see that Miranda and Charlie were in time for Cinema Club; avoid Oliver and any of his cronies who had stayed over.

During the night her phone had ended up in one of her fur-lined boots, switched off once she'd started her walk through the dark. She used it now to order a taxi for 9.15, ignoring the Messages sign. Half an hour would be ample for pulling herself together and getting dressed. She'd have a long, luxurious bath at home later, after her chores.

* * *

'Oh God, no!' she groaned as her cab drew up in the driveway behind her mother's blue BMW. She paid the driver and wound her coat protectively around her, fuming, but relieved to see that her own car was back from servicing. At barely two months old, it had developed an unaccountable oil leak.

She started to pull out her latchkey as the front door was whipped open.

'Where on earth have you been?' Carlotta demanded.

'Hello, Mum. Nice to see you too.'

'I asked where you were last night.'

'Yes, I heard you. What are you doing here?' She regretted the words the moment they were out. That was the prize invitation for a verbal dam-burst.

'What do you think I'm doing? How long did you think your baby-sitter was going to hang on while you made up your mind to come home? She left at eight this morning, and none too pleased. That goes for me too. I texted you. Didn't you get it?'

'Joanna rang you?' Damn her, making trouble in a fit of ill-humour. 'They aren't babies, Mum. They're nine and seven. So she's a *child*-minder. And anyway, Oliver should be around somewhere.'

'It seems he isn't.'

'Oh, really?' Her last brush with him had been to consign him to hell. Was it too much to hope he'd arrived there?

'Margot, you can't go on like this. The children were—' She was pumping spleen at full granny pressure.

'Ah, the children, yes. Are they dressed ready for

Cinema Club? Thank God my car's back. I need to drive them there. Sit yourself down, Mum. Relax over a nice cup of coffee while I'm gone. I shouldn't be long. We'll catch up on each other's news when I get back.'

As intended, it took the other's breath away, but only for an instant. 'We certainly will,' was the grim response.

She found the children in the morning room. Miranda was tearful and rebellious, having been forced by Granny to wash all the make-up off her face. Charlie was cowed. He hated anything approaching a row.

'Come on, kids,' Margot rallied them. 'Last in the car's a dingbat.'

'I can't go. Just look at me!' Miranda wailed. 'What'll my friends say? It's Saturday. I always try to look nice on a Saturday. They expect it of me.'

It wouldn't do any good to point out that her friends' opinions weren't worth a tinker's cuss: a lot of precocious show-offs aping adult sophistication. It was that overrated and expensive private school that encouraged them to compete like that. And Miranda was only nine. What must be expected when she hit thirteen?

'Mush, mush!' she ordered, shooing them ahead towards the outdoors. It raised a slow smile on Charlie's chubby little face as he recognised the language of husky-sledging. A good reader, recently he'd been tussling with a harrowing story of life in the Yukon.

They were early, and to avoid leaving them among the unruly queue at the barred doors, she drove a couple of circuits of the town, thankful that she'd managed to escape before her mother worked her into an unforgivable outburst. The encounter had been tedious enough, and there'd be more to endure when she got back, but by then they'd both have had time to cool off and adjust their positions.

Right, so Mother had rushed into the breach, as she saw it, but she needn't have implied that the children were being neglected. Normally arrangements were always made when both parents happened to be absent at the same time. But Carlotta – with a life empty of anything but Bridge with her elderly cronies and regular classical concerts at the Barbican or Festival Hall – seized every opportunity to imply she was indispensable, whereas the children had long grown out of a need for her and her old-fashioned strictures. Miranda's latest soubriquet for her, though voiced privately, was Old 54BC.

On her way back, Margot dropped off to buy a coffee and walnut gateau, Carlotta's favourite, from Katie's Pantry, in case the week's ravages had depleted all cake stocks at home. She re-entered the house falsely *con brio*, noted that her mother had sulked sufficiently not to have made herself coffee, and went to set up the espresso machine.

'What film will they be seeing?' Carlotta demanded from the sofa when Margot carried in the tray.

'Oh, something about an orphaned rabbit that found a new home,' Margot invented.

'I don't believe you even bothered to find out. God knows what dangerous rubbish these Hollywood people fill them up with nowadays.'

Well, not Pollyanna stuff, certainly. 'All right, *Rape on Main Street*, if you insist.' She just managed to indicate it was a joke, but its reception was frosty.

'How is your husband?' Carlotta enquired distantly after a short silence and some tinkling with her coffee spoon.

'His name is Oliver,' Margot reminded her.

Carlotta had refused to refer to him so familiarly since he'd left the BBC: sacked, as she preferred to see it, because of 'unacceptable public behaviour'.

'Has he managed to pick up a job somewhere else?'

'I wouldn't say he was looking very hard,' Margot admitted. There'd been no offers, his slow-developing slide from grace being well publicised. Once, Oliver Charrington had been a household name, the vibrant features presenter every channel wanted to poach. That was when she'd first met him, thrilled at being offered a seat at his table in the crowded BBC canteen. She'd never known what first attracted him to her, then a junior researcher in TV, working on the projected Decameron series.

She'd been ambitious, cultivated the relationship, eager to gain his support in her bid to train as a director. It was hardly her fault that once that was achieved, and she was taken on by an independent company in Maidenhead, she'd been diverted from drama to light entertainment: there'd been some very robust egos pushing in the queue ahead of her.

'So now the family must rely on what money you can bring in?'

'Which isn't *in*considerable.' Margot bridled at her derisive tone.

'But uncertain. How long can you hold down a position like that, with two children and a home to be responsible for? With your husband out of work in his fifties, suppose suddenly your job fell through too. This huge place must take a mint to run, especially with a weekday housekeeper and a carer for the children.'

How long? The implication was insulting, but long-term contracts were things Carlotta didn't understand. 'As long as I continue to build up my reputation, Mother, that's how long.'

'As he did. Cock of the walk once. And look at him now.'

A moody drunk and totally unmotivated, Margot agreed silently. Worse, he was a threat by contamination to her hard-won status. Signing her new surname so proudly in the church register ten years ago was now clearly proved an own goal. As she'd reckoned last night, Oliver had become excess baggage, at very best.

'It was a most unsuitable match. I never liked the man.' Carlotta's fork sliced viciously into the coffee and walnut gateau on her plate. 'There's something quirky about him, as though he's secretly laughing about something nobody else understands.'

Doesn't laugh a lot these days, Margot considered: just the occasional weak giggle over things that have turned out wrong. More often, when unaware of being observed, he looked in the depths of despair.

'You *could* divorce him, I suppose.' There was the hint of a sniff. 'Nobody in our family has ever needed recourse to that before, but at least you'd get half the property and of anything he still hasn't frittered away. Custody of the children, of course.'

36

Margot had sudden doubts. 'I'm not sure he wouldn't contest that.'

Carlotta made a noise almost as vulgar as a snort. 'No court would take him seriously. He's utterly inadequate as a parent. Not that you're impeccable yourself at present. How much time do you actually spend with them anyway?'

Margot ignored the question, not ready to cope with vulgar fractions.

'Everyone knows grandparents supply an important support function,' Carlotta mused aloud. 'There was an article about it in the *Telegraph* just recently. Demonstrating that I was here to back you up: that would surely make all the difference.'

Yes, with Carlotta guaranteeing the *demon* in demonstration. Margot's heart sank. Next, her mother would be demanding her own house-key, and there'd be no escaping her taking over.

There had to be an alternative. 'I suppose boarding school's always a possibility. I must start looking around,' she threatened.

'More expense. And that would involve splitting them up.'

'Why? There are co-educational places,' Margot snapped.

'Out of the question: even you must realise the risks inherent in that system: developing unsuitable relationships; teenage pregnancies. Oh no! We must insist on single-sex schools, whether boarding or not.'

We, Margot noted. Get rid of a husband and you're back

with Mother. Really, a sodden Oliver might be the lighter burden to bear.

Believing she had forcefully made her point, Carlotta started preparing to leave. Margot tightened her lips against offering lunch, recalling she'd missed sending her online weekly order for groceries. Now she must drive to Waitrose herself and lug it all back before picking up Miranda and Charlie from the film show.

With relief, she waved her mother's BMW out of the horseshoe driveway. Oliver's car still hadn't returned and his door to their double garage yawned open. Last night, after she'd refused their lift, the four men must have turned back to the West End and gone clubbing further, with probable disastrous consequences. Not that hangovers and emptied wallets were an unaccustomed blight to any of them. She doubted they'd have been chasing women: Oliver was oddly prudish in sexual matters. Poker was far more likely, though God alone knew what brains they had left to cope with that challenge.

The man sheltering in a doorway at the corner of Ladbroke Grove and Faraday Road moved a further step back, pulling the hood of his parka closer about his face. She was coming now, almost precisely at the expected time, purposefully crossing the main road, lithely dodging a red double-decker bus as she headed for the market in Portobello Road. He gave her fifty yards before falling in behind, lean shoulders hunched, fists thrust deep into his jeans pockets.

He recognised the same knee-length biscuit-coloured

puffer coat she often wore to work over her trousers, but today she also sported a bright green woolly hat topped with a bobble, under which the little hair left showing were streaks of flame across high cheekbones. There was no disguising her. It made following more easy; and she seemed unaware of anyone taking an interest. More than watching, he gloated. This was successful *stalking*.

The market stalls were enticingly laid out, striped awnings flapping in the biting wind. From somewhere nearby came a comforting aroma of roasting coffee beans, hot chestnuts and spicy grease from hotdogs and hamburgers. Beneath it, his sensitive nostrils picked up less pleasant smells from the milling crowd: the metallic scent of hands that had pawed over the fake jewellery, silver plate, saucepans, old books, superannuated toys. At one point he thought he caught the whiff of a blocked drain.

Ahead, the girl paused to examine a rail of wool and angora scarves, pulled down a purple one with fine turquoise stripes. *Go on, buy it*, he urged her silently, but after running it through her fingers she hung it carefully back with the others

Momentarily he lost her in a swirl of brash teenage girls, their arms linked across shoulders, loud-voiced and sexy, thrusting with bra-less boobs and pierced underlips as they flirted with the stallholder in hope of a mark-down. *Wannabe Spice Girls*, he thought. All that stuff was so passé. The group itself hadn't caught on so well the second time around.

He forged ahead and almost stepped on a mournful-eyed basset-hound, half hidden under a draped stall. It glared from bloodshot eyes before lurching off, tan-and-white undercarriage rhythmically swinging from side to side, almost sweeping the ground.

He continued, shouldering his way through the moving crowd until the green bobble hat reappeared ahead. He stood close behind her as she picked out silver dessertspoons from a junk stall, haggling for a reduction because they weren't a full set.

He recognised her scent: Chanel Allure. Not that she deliberately intended to attract. If anything she appeared unaware, even contemptuous, of any sexual effect she could exercise on others; existing in a sort of golden bubble, separate, uncontaminated. That was what made her different: she stood apart, vital in a very special way. At heart, passionate. He was sure of that. She was his unawakened golden girl.

Why would she be buying *five* spoons? he wondered. What little female clique did she intend serving a meal to? And where? He would soon know, because this time he was determined not to lose her but to hang on her scent until he found where she lived; enjoy casing the joint – wasn't that the term? And, most importantly, make sure that she lived alone.

The girl drifted on, waited while pitted green olives were weighed out for her, chose a tub of sun-dried tomatoes, shook her head at the offer of diced feta. Beyond the brightly stacked pyramids of fruit was the Flea Market. There most of the stalls were loaded with junk jewellery, watches of all ages and sizes, ceramics, paintings, antiquated cameras, period costumes, even a selection of dog collars ranging from brutal restrainers to diamante-studded bling.

The man continued to watch, curious over what interested her. How much of this stuff on sale was the product of thieving? Reputedly, the swag from country house break-ins was priced up and on display here within hours of being snatched. That was maybe what drew the crowds: if not something for nothing, at least get the nearest to it – something shady at a knockdown price. And mingling amongst those out for a bargain of possibly doubtful provenance were the watchful ones like himself. But they hadn't their sights on what he was after, more mundanely sent to trace missing valuables, pull in a suspected fence, collar yet another villain off the streets.

She was moving more purposefully now, heading for a small stall displaying exotic masks, dress combs, mantillas and veils. Amongst them, set up on pouting plaster heads, were half a dozen wigs. She lifted one off, so pale as to be almost white, removed her bobble hat and curtained her own gamine-cut, fiery hair with the straight blonde shower reaching down over her shoulder blades. In an instant she was gone. A totally different face seemed to peer out from the disguise. It distressed him, he felt cheated of his prey.

What could possess her to do that? Was she invited to some fancy dress party? Had she a secret life he as yet knew nothing of?

All the excitement of the chase had gone out of the morning as he stared at this ordinary girl, this nineteen-to-the-dozen slapper replicated everywhere now.

She wriggled the base of the wig, frowned at herself

from all angles in the mirror provided and peeled it off gently.

She had returned; was herself again.

He drew breath, realising how near-catatonic for an instant her transformation had made him. She was handing the wig across to have it wrapped; found the right notes in her purse to pay for the thing, and then consigned it to the deep hessian bag with the Shrek logo she carried on her arm.

She started to move away, smiling. The stallholder called her back to hand over the green bobble hat she'd left among the junk.

Silently, he followed. What else should he do?

Chapter Three

The leisurely soak with her favourite hypericum aromatherapy that Margot had promised herself on waking never happened. There hadn't even been time yet to take a quick shower. She felt scruffy in the same clothes she had gone to work in on the previous day.

She drove off to collect the children. Miranda complained at being left standing in the cold waiting to be picked up, and more loudly at being called back to help unload the weekly shopping when they reached home.

Oliver's cream Mercedes was now slewed across the other entrance to the driveway. It had a smashed left headlight and a dislodged front bumper. Their own gateposts and trio of Edwardian lamp standards appeared undamaged, so there would be reparations demanded by a third party. Not for the first time.

Margot refused to worry. That was what insurance companies and protected no-claims bonuses were for.

She assumed Oliver had survived with the luck of the devil and retired straight to bed. When eventually he awoke, he would likely have forgotten who'd brought him home.

Just herself and the children for lunch, in that case. She prepared ham salad and left the jacket potatoes to bake while she stripped off and turned on the shower in her bedroom. Before she'd quite finished dressing she heard piercing screams from downstairs. Charlie had heard the oven buzzer, smelt hot food and reached in to save the potatoes from burning. Fingers on both hands were scored with vivid red weals which needed plunging in cold water. He continued to sob in Margot's arms. Miranda had conveniently gone missing, having ignored instructions to set the lunch table.

I really don't deserve this, Margot swore to herself. But thank God Carlotta hadn't stayed on to witness this last disaster. On Monday, at school, Charlie's class teacher was sure to notice the burns and ring through. She might even consider informing Social Services.

When the boy's sore hands were loosely wrapped in gauze and his moans reduced to brave snuffles, Margot scraped the potatoes from the floor tiles, binned them and reached in the freezer for a couple of pizzas.

Their shared meal, eaten from trays in the lounge while watching television cartoons, was subdued, but at its end Miranda smugly claimed that Joanna would never have allowed them to do that.

'So what shall we do this afternoon?' Margot asked them. The plan had been to go swimming at the local fun pool, but for Charlie, still in pain, that was out of the question now.

'Would you like me to take you somewhere?'

They couldn't agree on that.

'Well, you've both got homework for school.'

'That's for Sunday.'

'We could swap over the days. Maybe Charlie will feel better tomorrow and we can go swimming then. Or how about the Model Village at Bekanscot?'

'That's kid's stuff,' Miranda condemned it loftily, 'and, anyway, you've forgotten it's closed in winter.'

They compromised with a walk into town to buy books, and Margot was determined on this occasion not to censor their choices. She bought a couple of crime paperbacks for herself, not that she'd have time to enjoy them. Offering her credit card for those and the children's selection, she found it was refused by the machine. She saw then that she'd brought the expired card by mistake and barely had change enough in her purse to cover their purchases. Now she had to mortgage time on Sunday to find the right card and draw money at a machine or she'd have nothing left for Monday.

They arrived home and the children mercifully disappeared, leaving Margot stretched on a sofa and dropping into sleep. When she awoke the room was dark and Oliver was standing in the doorway, silhouetted against the hall lights. He came in, wearing a striped, terry cloth dressing gown. His hair stood out in a wispy halo, dismally thinning and some colour between sandy and grey. His face looked crumpled. It irritated her to notice again how small he'd become lately.

'What are you doing?' he yawned.

'Trying to rest. Where are the children?'

'Swarming on my bed. We've been playing Draughts and Tri-Onimoes.'

45

'It's Tri-Ominoes.'

'Is it? Miranda's quite sharp at it. Good mental arithmetic.'

Margot slowly sat up. 'I'm glad she's good at something. She reminds me of Mother: always carping about something.'

'Charlie's hands are coming up in blisters.'

'Yes, well. Things happen.'

He wandered past her and stood moodily looking through the window, fists bunched in dressing-gown pockets. 'I assume you've had a hard week.'

Margot considered this. Taken all round, it was the part already spent here that had been the worst. 'And how was it for you?' she asked with heavy sarcasm.

'All right...ish'. He seemed to have lost interest in making conversation. She watched him drift out, heard him in the kitchen opening the refrigerator door, and then the clink of bottles. If by any chance he wanted food he could find it himself. Her next big challenge was to decide whether to get off her backside and turn on the lounge lights. The rest of the weekend yawned ahead without promise.

At work, Monday began badly. Greg Victor breezed in with pages of alterations. His assistant, Godfrey, a human ape in a lilac nylon sweatshirt through which his chest hairs pricked like three-day stubble, started handing out script changes to everyone. Margot accepted hers by one corner. Her heart sank even before she noticed her name on it had been misspelled, the 'r' changed to 'g' so that it

46

read as 'Maggot'. Probably something more than a mere typo.

She was already feeling heated over Marion Harmer's ridiculous insistence on a mention in the credits. 'Maybe in the final run,' she had conceded at last, 'after we've given you a line or two to say.' How else could she be named – as Woman Frying Sausages, background, at the Greasy Spoon Caff?

Marion had gone off in a huff, growling under her breath about ringing her agent. Getting even a wallpaper part had given her *illusions de grandeur.* Margot silently prayed she hadn't already been pecking at Greg and squeezed a one-line speech out of him. That was a problem, the personal politicking that went on behind one's back. But no, Marion wasn't Greg's type, if indeed he had one.

She watched as the executive producer took the floor, running a thin hand through his disarrayed blond hair. 'Blah, blah, blah,' he said. 'Just a few more quips here for Timmy while they're struggling with the ladders. Cut out the bit about running over the cat they've just rescued. Seems that's an old tale told in every fire station that ever there was: utterly groan-worthy. Then Roger – where the devil is Roger? – God, man, go and put your head under a cold tap. I want you bright-eyed and bushy-tailed for a spot of sparky with the housewife next-door. I hope you appreciate we've been up half the night revising this script for you; not getting legless in some downriver dive like some. We're giving her a bit more with the rescued children. Jamie, you got that new interior organised? Ok, then we'll start with that in half an hour. Meanwhile, everyone read through their alterations and be ready to follow on. Right?'

Presumably that question includes me? Margot asked herself sourly. Before Friday's location shoot at Fulham, she had already booked the studio here for the next run-through, starting with the set for the pub where the retained firemen gathered after a shout. Now, with Greg's suggested switch, Hattie at Wardrobe would have to put the men back into working gear instead of their sweaty string vests and civvy jackets. Unless she stood her ground, pointing out that the sequences were settled and agreed. There was no room for contingency adjustment. She took a deep breath.

'Sorry, Greg. That's not on. It's past rehearsal stage on the scenes you want changed. We'll have to start over again here, and you know studio time's costly. They'll need time to learn any script changes and practise, so eleven at the earliest for the inserted scene. Anyway, we have a booked run-through in ten minutes.'

For a second he faced her open-mouthed, then, with a wave of the bundled papers in his right hand, he indicated the door to his office. 'A word in your ear, Margot,' he hissed. 'You could be getting your sequences sadly in a twist; if nothing else more intimate.'

'Take five then, everyone,' she shouted, and watched them disperse to the tea bar before following Greg out. It gave just long enough to fight down the flush threatening to rise up her neck and suffuse her cheeks. At least her voice hadn't wobbled. She was still the director they called Ice Matron.

'I won't have it,' Greg started on her, once the door was closed behind them.

'Have what?' she asked coolly.

'You undermining my authority in front of the others.'

'Just directing, like I'm paid to do, Greg. I've never challenged you as producer. Wouldn't dream of it. You're the boss. There are just practicalities to consider. Time and space things. Costs, of course.' Bring up the subject of money and he hadn't a case: it was his everlasting theme. Second, of course, to magnifying his own importance.

He faced her suspiciously but could pick up no sarcasm in her expression. 'Remember, Margot, I'm here to guide you, advise you when things get a bit tight. To *support* you, Margot. Can't you appreciate how good I am for you?'

She looked blankly back. If she were really truthful she'd admit, yes, you are. You've managed to put me off men for all time. And why does everyone want to support me, when all I need is a free hand?

She brandished the script amendments. 'This new thing for Roger. Is he just having a fling with the neighbour-woman or developing a real relationship? I mean, how far is it intended to go?'

'You'll have to thrash out the details with the writers. We need to build up a bit of romance for him before he finally gets the push.'

'The push?'

'The man's a liability, Margot; taking uppers and downers all the time. I caught him in the bog snorting a line last week. He looks like shit, but the public still have a soft spot for the character. So we soften him up over the next few scenes, and then tragedy strikes, boom-boom. The pathos thing. Get all the mums in the audience dabbing at their eyes.'

'Kill him off? A fatal blaze? This is meant to be light entertainment, Greg.'

'That doesn't rule out drama. You've got to have suspense. Excitement and sex, to pump up the ratings. You know that's what counts.'

She did. And heavier drama was what she knew she could do. But could poor Roger stretch to it? And how would it go down with Them Upstairs?

'It'll mean appointing a new station officer for future series,' she cautioned. 'Who do we promote? Or do we bring in a new face?'

'Work in a spot of suspense there. Meanwhile, try them all out. But no need for Roger to know we're looking for a substitute. Not yet.'

There's no chance it can be kept under our hats, Margot thought. For gossip, this place is like a leaky colander. Give way and I'll have made another enemy. There's bound to be trouble.

'Get our legal eagle to go over the small print in his contract,' she warned him. 'Anyway, my five minutes are up now. I'm needed on set.' She nodded curtly and let herself out.

In the tea bar she entered a changed atmosphere. Three scriptwriters were in a huddle at one of the plastic tables, firing additions and amendments at each other in an uneasy mixture of rebellion and competitive hysteria. At least one of them must already have spent half the night with Greg, preparing to thrust this particular cat among the pigeons. Best leave them to it while she rallied her actors for the next scene.

Their conversation cut off expectantly at her approach, and she turned an icy glance at their curious faces. 'Set three,' she announced, 'as planned: window corner of the Jolly Ratcatcher pub.'

Guessing ahead that Margot's arguments would prevail, Jenny Barnes had already herded the cast towards the three-walled set. They seated themselves round a window table in the mock-up ancient pub.

The story ran that their station had been full-time before threat of closure in a government economy drive. However, local bigwigs' pressure and several spectacular street protests had gained a part reprieve so that it was now served by part-time retained firemen called in for emergencies by pager. All of them were employed locally as artisans, shopkeepers or tradesmen pledged to drop their work when a shout came through. Their proud boast was a four-minute turnout. They rather played up their roles as Shakespearian comics, but were regarded in the Jolly Ratcatcher as minor celebrities and heroes.

The upper half of Kathy Richards, playing the publican's wife and purveyor of streetwise wisdom, could be seen, left, leaning on the far side of the bar. She dusted off her plump elbows and faced up to Margot. 'I 'ope yor not 'avin' a lot more of that effin' steam in 'ere todye. I jes' 'ad me 'air done.'

'Very nice it looks too,' Jenny put in.

Timmy the Twit chirruped up, 'Going someplace

special tonight then, Kathy? Didn't think you were one for clubbing.'

'It's me daughter-in-law's burfdye, that's what, and I ain't 'aving 'er looken down on me. So I treated meself to a perm.'

'Well, unless we're incorporating that little exchange into the script, guys, let's go through it the way it is,' Jenny suggested. She turned to Margot. 'Nothing's been changed for this scene, thank heaven, so it's a clear run.'

'I cudda done with a little more to say,' Kathy regretted. 'So if it ends a coupla minutes short, you know 'oo to ask.' She turned to produce a tray crammed with plates of Caesar salad, slamming it down on the bar. ''Ere you are, lads! 'Ealthy eating, like wot that fire chief of yors threatened you with. And anyone 'oo isn't knocking the weight orff and would rather 'ave one of me steak and kidney puds is welcome.'

Margot nodded to Jenny, who collected her script from the table and retreated into the background. 'Right,' Margot announced, climbing towards the gallery.

'Jamie; when you're ready.' Her disembodied voice sounded in the floor manager's headset.

'On cue,' he commanded. 'Set three, scene six, take one. Five, four, three...' His fingers continued the countdown.

As he swung the mike's boom towards Kathy, who was now to repeat her opening lines, George Bullock was conscious of the director above and behind him in the gallery, eyes glued to her monitors. One of the advantages, as well as drawbacks, of being on the Sound team was that you weren't noticed. Vital, yes, but compared with

Vision, Sound was the poor relation, with him recognised as a human attachment only if, through a combination of gravity and an actor's long-windedness, his mike dropped into the shot. He swung the boom to catch Roger's pompous putdown speech and the sneaky little titter from Timmy the Twit. Kathy, her salads rejected, sniffed and retired with her tray towards the kitchen area, out of shot.

He followed the chaotic dialogue as 'the lads' organised a whip-round and raised seventeen pounds thirteen pence towards a round of pizzas to go with their pints while Roger feigned deafness. 'Babe' Newson was entrusted with collecting the dosh and offering later settlement for the shortfall since the shout had caught him in his overalls and strapped for cash. He disappeared, slamming out through the mock-up door to the left. The frame and plywood fabric vibrated, but the bang was non-existent. There'd need to be a sound effect added there. Nobody in direction would be bothered. Yesterday, on location, there'd been that bloody jumbo jet overhead. Thank God Jenny had insisted on a retake. But Margot had been difficult. The bitch took Sound for granted and begrudged any halting of the takes.

Jenny, now she was different. Jenny even seemed to recognise there were human beings out on the floor making the magic work. He'd just missed a seat next to her in the canteen van last night, that slimy sod Nicco had beaten him to it by a whisker, shaking his black curls at her and grinning like an ape.

That one needed watching. He'd already grabbed old Walter by the short and curlies, sucking up to Margot when the senior camera was away at his retirement seminar. Now she'd only ears for what her new man had to suggest. It was OK him upstaging his boss and shinning up to the façade platform with a lightweight camera on his shoulder, but toting a boom and full Sound gear up there had been out of the question. So guess who'd had to go up and fix personal mikes in the kids' clothing? The result wasn't quality, and would have to be enhanced.

The eating scene continued with some argy-bargy and a few flat jokes, but there wasn't much for him to do once he'd fixed a shared mike in the pottery mug, central table, until Kathy was due to return just out of range. He fell back, resting his arms, and stared round to check on positions. There had only been room for camera one on this scene.

In the gallery, all interest was directed to the bank of monitors, but Jenny was down here watching the set. 'Oh God,' she groaned, as one of the pizzas, under attack from a blunt knife, leapt off the table and skidded across the floor. 'Cut,' she snapped into her mike.

'That's the point. The bloody thing won't,' came the complaint from the actor involved.

'No,' Margot countermanded from on high, 'I like it. Scramble for the thing, dust it off and return it to the plate. Nice bit of slapstick available there. They wouldn't have let it go to waste.'

'You expect us to eat it now?' Roger demanded.

"Elf and Safety,' somebody moaned. 'The man's never there when you need him. Next we'll have half the cast down with food poisoning!'

Chapter Four

Toby Frobisher handed in his black, velvet-collared Crombie, adjusted his cuffs and made his way to the bar. It was barely twelve, and there weren't many in yet, but he made out Oliver Charrington slumped over a table in the far corner. His companion was a stout, middle-aged woman with wire-wool hair, who was leaning forward to catch his every word. But Oliver apparently had nothing to say.

Uncertain what he might be walking into, Toby passed across their line of vision without making any sign of recognition and ordered a Martini. Oliver was more alert than he'd seemed, lifting a hand and looking unmistakably relieved. Toby went across and suffered an introduction.

'Er, Toby, this is Ms...' He glanced down at the card on the tabletop between his single malt and her grenadine. 'Ms Helanie Towers.'

Toby expressed his pleasure and took her plump hand in his. She was wearing a number of chunky rings set with serious stones. 'M'friend Toby,' Oliver offered unnecessarily. 'Ms, er, Towers has just completed the script for a TV play,' he explained sadly. 'And she doesn't know what to do with it.'

Owlishly he reconsidered his words and suspected they hadn't sounded complimentary. 'That is, she would like to know how to go about getting it on screen,' he corrected.

Toby considered, and rejected, saying that she had come to the right person for information. Clearly Oliver wanted out of this situation.

'That's a very unusual name,' Toby substituted. 'Helanie: I don't think I've ever come across that before.'

The woman dimpled. 'I had two wealthy grannies,' she confided. 'One Helen and the other Annie. It seemed a good idea when it came to my christening; and it hasn't served me badly over the years.'

'So what is the theme of your play? Comedy, tragedy, soap?'

She turned on him with fulsome gratitude.

'Actually,' he rushed to forestall her, 'television is completely unknown territory to me, although I enjoy a play with a good storyline when I'm relaxing.'

'It's about the south of France,' she gushed. 'Marseille, in fact. There's an American warship visiting the harbour and the local girls are all wild to go aboard and be entertained. Well, of course, there are complications, especially when one of them meets a sailor who turns out to be the son of a long-lost uncle who was believed to have been killed years ago in Saigon.'

Toby nodded, trying to date the play. When exactly were Frenchmen getting themselves killed in Saigon? Or maybe it was an ongoing situation. A cautious traveller, he suspected the Far East could be dodgy that way.

The woman went on revealing plot details. She was quite right about there being complications.

Suddenly Oliver recovered his courage and broke in. 'If you have a three-page synopsis ready prepared, you could always send it to the script department of one of the better TV companies and ask if they'd like to see it.'

The woman looked horrified. 'Oh, I would never do that! I've been warned about script departments, how they reject stuff out of hand, and then six months later out comes your work almost word for word under someone else's name! I'd need to take out protection first, something like a patent.'

'Copyright,' Toby corrected her. 'Get it published in book form first.'

'Maybe I should. Only it's a play, you see. That would be an awful lot of work, rewriting it as narrative.'

'But so worthwhile,' Toby wickedly pursued.

She smiled greedily on him. 'You're not by any chance a publisher?'

'Nothing so distinguished. Just my friend's doctor. And I've simply dropped in to make sure he gets something healthy for his lunch.'

Oliver was again reduced speechless, aghast at her forthright damning of script departments.

Toby started to rise. 'So, if you'll excuse us—'

'What did I do to deserve that?' Oliver asked weakly as they progressed towards the dining room. 'A horrendous woman. And you know I never eat at midday.'

'You're going to get something solid in you today to

mop up the liquid that's almost audibly sloshing inside. I'm getting tired of warning you that alcohol delays any progress you could make.'

He watched the familiar discontent settle over his friend's face and changed the subject. 'How on earth did you get involved with this Helanie person?'

Oliver shrugged hopelessly. 'She recognised me from old magazine photographs; came barging through the door and said someone had told her she'd be sure to find me in here.'

'You often are. I took the same chance myself, to ask how you finally got home on Friday.'

'Oh, that. The other chap drove me, I think. Not old Badger, because we'd dropped him off earlier, soon after you. Said he had to put his trumpet to bed. Yes, I remember now. It was the jazz fan we picked up at Ronnie Scott's. But by Amersham he ran the Merc into a traffic island and flattened the bollard. Then he panicked and must have run off, left me stranded. I woke up mid-morning parked on the A413 and drove myself home.'

Almost full marks for recall, Toby noted. So Oliver hadn't been as far gone as he'd seemed at the time; maybe just slumped in depression, exhausted after the high of the music they'd listened to. A fine doctor he was to have abandoned him like that, but there were times when patients of Oliver's kind got even him down; and exercising the necessary authority was inexcusable in company.

He pushed the menu under the other man's nose. 'Choose, Oliver, or I shall do it for you.'

'I told you. I don't want anything. I'd choke.'

'They're doing Dover sole in a lemon and honey sauce, with creamed potato and petits pois. That sounds bland enough. On the bone could be too fiddly for you. I'll see that they fillet it. And watercress soup to begin with. I'll be having duck pate followed by roast lamb with baked peppers and shallots.'

'Do you eat as much every day?'

'A restaurant-cooked lunch, yes. It saves slaving over a microwave in the evening. I get by then on fruit, nuts and sorbet.'

'Sounds hideously healthy.'

'It's the price of living alone. There's no cherished little woman to fuss over me, like some have.'

This plunged Oliver into such a mood of silent introspection that Toby at once regretted the flippant words. Recalling Margot's behaviour on Friday night, when she'd waved them all contemptuously off, he feared it had signalled the start of a stormy weekend.

And yet shouldn't that have cleared the air? Instead, he suspected, his friend had bottled up his wounded feelings over the public rebuff, leaving the situation unsorted. He still had the ability to walk away and anguish in private, certainly when it came to dealing with Margot.

The others hadn't been really stinking drunk, mostly elated after an evening of superb trad jazz. Oliver went manic, demanding to be driven to pick his wife up from the location shoot in Fulham. Small wonder he suddenly hit rock bottom at the scathing reception. Not helpful for a bi-polar subject.

Now he was so absorbed by private thoughts that he had

started automatically spooning up his soup and wolfing the hot garlic section of baguette that accompanied it. Toby left him to it. When the main course arrived, Oliver became suddenly aware of his surroundings and pushed the plate away.

'Trouble is,' he mumbled miserably, 'I love her, you see. Always have done, always will. She is pretty damn marvellous, you know.'

Poor devil, lusting after the unattainable, Toby thought, because 'Treat 'em mean to keep 'em keen' was the ploy of most dominant women. Except that lusting wasn't really in Oliver's line. He'd even accepted the segregated bedrooms her demanding work apparently required, being a man who'd be more grateful for an occasional warm hug than revelling in sexual athletics. And Margot? Simply not bothered one way or the other. Had she ever felt real love for her husband? Was there room in that woman for anything so consuming, outside her career? Even then, Oliver should have confided his condition to her. Safeguarding his patients' privacy prevented Toby putting that right.

And Oliver, refusing to see that the relationship was past mending, was equally blind to the needs of the standby friend whose own marriage had so tragically ended.

'Eat your fish and I'll order you a glass of chilled Montrachet with it,' Toby persuaded.

It was like wheedling a small child into swallowing its breakfast, Oliver thought. He'd had to do that at one time with Miranda, when she was stick-thin and missing her mummy, who always dashed off, unfed, to work.

'What would I do without you to bully me?' he asked.

Good old Toby was the one constant thing you could rely on, always around when needed, ever since – at thirteen and both dumped forlornly at boarding-school – they'd shared the same dormitory, and later a study, sometimes escaping before sun-up in their final summer, with rod, line and net, to go secretly fishing in the Dart.

The unexpected food had had a cheering effect on Oliver. By the time they were in a taxi and halfway to the clinic he was rattling on about some fantastic short story he'd read in a magazine at the barber's.

'That's the sort of thing Margot should be working with, not the present rubbish. It was – just, well surreal: about this sweet country girl who came to London for a job interview and got picked up in a bar by some guys who introduced her to smoking skunk and…'

'So she was a cigarette smoker already? If not, she'd probably have choked. That would be jumping into the deep end, surely?'

Oliver frowned. 'You're not listening, Toby. She was in a bar, drinking; not in a swimming pool.'

'You can't smoke in bars any more. It's illegal. They'd have to go outside and do it in the street.' He was getting irritated by all this irrelevant matter.

'*Do* it? I hadn't got to that bit yet. You see, she hadn't any idea – these guys, see? Well, then she just started feeling unwell, and…'

'I'm afraid that story's been done. Over and over.'

Oliver rounded on him, almost tearful. 'You know your trouble? You've got no imash-imagination.'

'I don't need imagination. I'm a psychiatrist. I'm dealing with the rape-drug situation and its resultant trauma every day of my working life, Oliver.'

'Well, you needn't be so unfriendly about it. Anyway, where're we going? Tell the cabbie Marylebone. I need to get a train home. Damned car's gone to be mended. I'm sure I told you that. Why don't you ever listen to me?'

'We're heading for the clinic. I've got afternoon surgery. You're coming along for a check-up. Have a little nap there and you'll feel fine.'

Oliver shrank back into his corner, eyes squeezed shut. He bunched his fists and stayed silent until the taxi decanted them before the steps to the colonnaded Institute. Toby paid the cabbie and slid an arm under his friend's elbow.

'I don't have to do what you say.'

'That's right. You don't. Just to please me, eh?'

Oliver followed him past the smiling receptionist, into the lift, up one floor, along the corridor, through the waiting room – empty except for a young woman almost identical to the one downstairs – and into Toby's consulting rooms.

'I need a pee,' he said, and walked past Toby into the toilet, where he sat on the pedestal and put his head in his hands. He seemed to have re-enacted all of this so many times, and nothing ever got any better. There'd be tests and an injection and he wasn't ready for it yet. He knew he'd been silly again, really rude, and he'd have to tell Toby how sorry he was.

* * *

Nicco had been acting modestly all morning and keeping out of old Walter's line of sight. When a convenient break came and the older man was caught up in conversation with George Bullock from Sound, he awaited his moment and brought two beakers of coffee across. 'Milk and three sweeteners, right?' he asked, smiling.

Walter took the beaker without acknowledging it, turned a shoulder and continued speaking. 'Like you say, Sound does get less consideration than Vision. It has to, especially on location. It's a case of seize the day, the light, the action. But you've plenty of back-up in post-production. For us, if there's a dud run it means shooting the whole thing over again.'

'No need for that on the fire scenes,' Nicco commented, entering the conversation. 'I got an early look at the rushes. Sound and Vision both perfect.' He displayed his equally perfect teeth. The two men looked at him and then at each other. The little group broke up.

No sweat, Nicco told himself: he'd offered a peace pipe and the old chap had chosen to ignore it. Not that it mattered a barn owl's hoot. Walter was as good as gone already. There were others he could more profitably exercise his charm on.

Even as he thought this, Margot appeared on the set floor, frowning over a clipboard in one hand. She looked up to encounter the full power of his smile. 'Ah, Nicco,' she said, startled.

'Quite a morning,' he said. 'Not easy for anyone, especially you.'

She looked slightly embarrassed at the personal tone,

and it encouraged him. There was a red stain running up her neck. He wondered if it was a menopausal flush or due to his own presence. He was intuitive about women and he caught now a certain frisson of excitement off her. It wasn't mere professional pleasure in having discovered a new, enterprising protégé who could contribute to her successes. No: there was more.

'That scene we inserted on location...' She hesitated, unable to continue.

'Using the lightweight camera on the kids?' he helped out.

'Yes.'

But it wasn't just that scene. A more disturbing frame formed a double exposure on her mind. The half-dream, half-idle thought, as she had slid into sleep on Friday night returned to her: the ridiculous image of this young man as a romantic hero. Whatever had got into her? He was Second Camera, that's all; just one of her technical team.

She forced herself to be rational and meet his eyes. They were large, brilliant, the iris and pupil so dark that they were indistinguishable.

List the rest of him, she told herself impatiently, to establish some detachment: the short-sleeved cotton shirt that shrieked High Street store; the tight blue jeans, unpressed and slightly shabby; the scuffed, once-white trainers with turned-up toes; and the body within all this. No, just don't go there!

'Would you,' she almost stammered, 'like to get me a coffee?'

'How do you like it?' Somehow the question sounded a

little indecent. She was amazed at herself, how inadequate she felt, so unprepared.

'With milk?' he was coaxing her.

'A little. No sweetener.'

He smiled that wide, white display of perfect teeth.

Other figures came between as he loped away, but something about him lingered, a sort of promise that there was more to follow. Promise – or was it *threat*?

In sudden panic she knew she didn't need this. Even as his back disappeared, she turned on her heel and walked rigidly away.

Chapter Five

Jenny Barnes, usually shadowing Margot during breaks in case something crucial came up, had taken her coffee across to Athene, the production assistant. She'd found no chance to speak with her before, and her excitement needed to spill out. 'I've got it! Picked it up Sunday and it's fantastic,' she announced.

'That's great, Jenny. Did you ride it in this morning?'

'Yup. Traffic was a bit hairy at first, mostly filtering through London, but once I was out on Western Avenue I got the chance to open her up. She's wonderfully nippy for weaving among the bigger stuff.'

'Well, don't end up as a traffic statistic.'

'I'm not that crazy.' Jenny grinned. 'It's a relief not having to rely on lifts anymore.'

'I guess so, but I'm surprised you don't follow the trend and move out this way. Rents are cheaper and the air's cleaner.'

'I'm not a country girl like you. London still has a lot going for me. I get my daily social fix there. And nightly.' She grinned and closed one eye.

Athene was watching the general move back into position to resume the run. 'Got to go, I'm afraid.' She turned back when she'd gone a couple of steps. 'How's Margot this morning?'

'All right, I think. Why?'

'I thought she looked sort of...I don't know. Off-balance. A tad unsure of herself.'

'I've been too busy watching the action to notice her. But I'll make a point of it.'

If Margot was flagging, there was an opening there for herself: she was more than ready to fill any breach, never missing a chance to get in first with something that would go down well with Greg. She took her seat on the set and was ready when the director passed to climb to the gallery.

Margot looked as she ever did, her pale, shiny skin stretched tightly over the bony face, deep-set eyes wary; no feverish flush or trembling hands. Yet Athene was more often than not right with her observations. She had the eyes of a hawk and remarkable acuity. She had quickly picked up on Jenny's relationship with Jamie, and understood that on her side it went no deeper than a need for free transport. Well, that necessity was over now. But not the doubt that in other directions Athene might pick up more than was good for her.

During the next break Athene went down to the studio floor, passing behind a group of lighting and camera crew. Jamie was among them, with a floor plan open in his hands. She wondered if he knew yet about Jenny's bike. She might well not have bothered to warn him there'd be a cut-off in her requirements – and to his reciprocal comforts. He passed for an unflappable sort of guy, but she knew that the surface impression hid a flash temper which surged if his requirements weren't met. Jenny could be at risk if she expected to drop him like an overheated plate of spaghetti. He could assume she was his property from habit.

Before Margot settled at her bank of monitors, she looked down from the glass wall of the gallery to the set rigged for the new scene Greg had inserted. Roger was about to launch on his revised script, setting his cap at the motherly neighbour in her kitchen. During the break she'd done a quick read-through with them both, with Athene timing it to four minutes and three seconds. Roger was weaker in a romantic role, rather than a bluff one. The woman clearly wasn't his type.

Sexual attraction was a weird business. She had never understood what first compelled Oliver to pursue her, the only man she had ever slept with. She'd read somewhere that in every relationship one partner was more involved than the other, and that seemed to make sense. In her own case she accepted that she'd never really needed a man as such.

At school, she'd marvelled at the giggly preoccupation of her peers with smutty affairs. She'd had no time for boys' clumsy gropings, too busy with getting grades, and later a good degree to give access to a rewarding career. That was the first point at which males had begun to matter, because they controlled entrée to the jobs she coveted. Although she'd felt worthy of success through ability alone, Oliver's besotted courtship had come as a surprising bonus. His interest in her at that time had opened doors.

There was nothing wrong with sex when eventually experienced, but it had been a required condition, like setting up a home, having children: a byway to security while she concentrated on the more important things in life. There had been no place for passion. She had hardly been aware of its existence – until now, this sudden shattering doubt that there was a dimension she had missed out on.

Central on the studio floor, Jamie was pointing out markings and checking the actors' positions, but the camera and Sound crews blocked out the set, their equipment forming a wall in between. Even then he was half a head taller than any of them. Old Walter clambered onto camera one's crane and crouched over his viewfinder. Camera two was set up left of him, for a wide shot on the same scene. Nicco's slim spine was erect, his weight balanced lightly on both feet in their dilapidated trainers. His face was hidden behind the glossy black curls. Watching him as he mounted his mobile camera, she was reminded of a waiter who had served at their table when her father took her as a child to Cyprus. From the rear his long, bunched hair had hung down like a glossy doorknocker over brown shoulders swelling under a translucent white shirt.

So, subliminally, had she been attracted to the Mediterranean type even so young – foreshadowing this mid-life revelation of what might have been?

She spoke into her mike, audible to all on the floor below. 'Stand by, Studio. We're running up to record,' She saw the young man turn to glance up at her. She couldn't return his smile: it was too devastating. She felt as though everyone must be staring at her, defenceless at the window. She turned to face the monitors, slid into her seat, buzzed Jamie to signal the start of recording. Over her loudspeaker she picked up his voice announcing the scene and take, counting down, 'Five, four, three...'

A recording without full rehearsal: Margot gritted her teeth and silently cursed Greg for fiddling with the sequences. The changes were unlikely to rescue the show from its present level of tedium.

The London taxi Toby had ordered for Oliver decanted him in his driveway at 4.10 p.m., too late for him to pick up the children from school. Joanna would be doing it by now. The daytime carer's car was missing from in front of the door.

Time for a snifter before they all returned, Oliver told himself comfortably. Then his friend's warnings about alcohol warring with the drugs kicked in. Dear old Toby. So maybe he'd miss out on this top-up, make a sort of Lent sacrifice, even in November, because Toby thought it mattered. By now nothing was likely to make much difference to a lost soul like himself, but one had to stay mannerly as long as one could.

There was a pile of post waiting on the hall table. He guessed most of it would be for Margot, except some junk mail from insurance companies, prosthetic manufacturers and bespoke footwear retailers who still considered him important enough to ply for his custom. He passed it all by, making for his study. There he headed for the decanters, lifted the cut-glass stopper from the scotch, sniffed it and religiously replaced it. To show he could.

What next? Go horizontal, he supposed. He trailed upstairs, having set up an ancient looped recording of Bowie, turned loud enough to reach his room if the door was left open. As a further salute to Toby he removed most of his clothes, but dropped them on the floor. The under-sheet in his single bed struck cold as he pulled the duvet over bare shoulders.

'Sleep,' he told himself. At least that was one thing he could still do with no trouble, thanks to the regular doses of amitryptyline. He was on a real cocktail of drugs by now. If they were all so successfully mind-changing he wondered how much of his original self remained. And if any did, who but himself would miss the old chap?

No, do as Toby said: think happy thoughts as you slide into sleep. Toby, who was always so right, hadn't changed since that first confusing plunge into boarding-school existence. Because of their friendship there were good memories from those days, however desperate he'd been because of separation from his father.

But he'd worked doggedly through to sixth form and then university; thrown himself into creative television. And become a success. Oh, those glorious days when he'd made really good programmes that got top ratings, skimming off all those awards. It was at this peak that he'd met Margot, wooed and won her. Perhaps he'd been too much on top of the world then, already into a hyper-manic phase. Had his euphoria been only a symptom of what was later in store for him?

Happy memories, but all in the past. He wished he could believe happiness was possible ahead. What made someone like Toby able to carry on, confident but quite alone after Molly and their baby were killed, able to provide the stability his patients lacked on their own? Strong genes, supposedly. Whereas his own... He'd never confided in Margot about that, although the press hadn't been able to leave it alone. There were things too awful to share with her.

Happy thoughts, he reminded himself; and here he was beginning to wallow again in one of his miseries. Scared, he hid his head under the bedcovers and felt tears pricking out between his tightly pressed eyelids. Nothing would save him. He had flared and burnt out. He was going to turn into a nutter like his father.

Greg Victor's inserted scene was suffering hiccups all the way. After three or four corrections from Margot in tones of barely suppressed despair, as Roger either mumbled his lines or delivered them sergeant-major style, she withdrew, leaving it to Jenny down on the floor, to try inserting some spirit into his pursuit of the comely housewife. He would clearly have preferred to make the effort with a teenage blonde bimbo, and his smirky technique was that of a night-club pick-up rather than tender attraction.

Greg, origin of these difficulties, also gave up and disappeared from the studio. In the tea bar the scriptwriters again had their heads grimly together over their laptops, and were planning rebellion. By the time Margot called a break everyone was thoroughly browned off.

Nicco collected two coffees and carried them up to the gallery, since she had refused to come down on the set. 'I dropped a spot of brandy in, from my emergency kit,' he told her, grinning, 'as liquid defibrillation.' He leant casually in the doorway, ankles crossed.

'Smart diagnosis,' she said wryly, reaching for the beaker. A sudden smile broke out. 'You know alcohol's not allowed up here.'

'I won't tell on you.' His smile was puckish.

They sipped in silence. 'Roger can't do it,' Nicco finally commented.

'He has to try. Greg's building him up for a dramatic drop-out.'

'You make it sound as though it's the chop.'

'It is. This was to be his final redemption, but he's out of his depth, can't rise to it.' She didn't know why she was discussing this with a mere cameraman, but it was a relief to let it out. 'Discretion,' she cautioned him, finger on lips. 'He doesn't know we're killing him off.'

'Our secret,' he assured her wickedly.

This was all right, she thought, watching him through half-closed eyes. She could manage at this badinage level. What she must avoid was revealing the intense effect he exercised on her. It destroyed her defences: something she wasn't used to. Somehow she had to stay in charge.

'Tell me about yourself,' she heard herself demanding.

He was unsurprised, spun a chair and straddled it. 'Not a long story. I'm twenty-four, live in Chesham with my parents. Dad's a chef. He's Italian by birth, from an

74

enormous family in Perugia. Mother's a nurse. I've an older sister, Violetta, a gorgeous brunette airhead.'

'That's them. What about you? Any hobbies?'

'I read a lot, go surfing in the summer, like cooking. Actually, I can knock up quite a good three-course meal. I half-own a narrowboat on the Regent's Canal with a chap I was at school with. Jolyon's a rising barrister in Grays Inn.'

'I'm impressed. So what school turned out a cameraman and a barrister?'

'Wycombe Royal Grammar. Where did you go?'

She hadn't expected that, and hesitated. 'An inner London comprehensive,' she admitted. 'And before you ask, yes, it was tough. I got bullied until I learnt to stand up for myself. And I did get into Cambridge.'

'That accounts for it.'

For what? she questioned silently. Well, obviously he thought she'd become a bully in her turn.

'So look at you now,' he approved.

It was almost time work resumed. Margot looked up at the clock and he took the hint, removing the beakers as he left.

Before they started up again, Margot had another word with Roger, flattered him into almost believing he could make something of the new scene. 'Your audience is already with you; you're the man who holds the fire crew together, their heroic boss. This is a new dimension they're going to be let in on. Your tender side.'

'Heroic? That's a joke. I'm playing a bossy, fall-flat-on-my-arse part.' Roger was being unusually honest. 'It's pathetic. Even Timmy has better lines with his bloody puns.'

'So show us what else you're capable of. This mumsie woman, give her something to get doe-eyed over: Mister Wonderful. But she's shy, and you have to go after her. Gently, though. You make her feel she's a teenager again. All the middle-aged mums in the audience are going to fall for you as well.'

She turned to Jenny, 'Anything to add?'

'Look her straight in the eyes when you're speaking, and stand firm on your legs. No lover's convincing if he stands with bent knees.'

He flinched and looked away.

Damn, Margot thought. She needn't have been so scathing. Must I have a word with her as well? The bloody girl's getting above herself. She'll want my job next.

The run-through proceeded a little better. The techs had mastered the script changes and Greg kept safely out of the way. It wasn't perfect, and they'd spent all afternoon on it, but Margot felt that tonight they could risk recording that scene and go on to Greg's next insertion for the pub scene when Roger was ribbed by his men over his new lady love.

She packed her bundle of scripts in her briefcase, picked up her laptop and went out to her car. Across the yard she saw Nicco getting into a new-looking little red Fiesta. He didn't appear to see her, and drove off with considerable panache.

'Gigolo,' she muttered under her breath.

* * *

76

At home she found Joanna had put out some covered dishes for everyone's supper, but as she sat down with the children the front-doorbell sounded. 'I'll go,' Charlie offered.

'Not after dark. You don't know who it could be.' She pushed him back on his chair and went through to peer at the CCTV screen in the kitchen.

It was Toby Frobisher. She hoped he wouldn't be expecting a meal.

He stood hesitantly on the step as she opened up. 'Is Oliver in, by any chance?'

Like a school kid, wanting his buddy to come out and play, Margot thought. 'I guess so,' she told him vaguely. 'He'll be somewhere about.' Joanna wouldn't have left the children alone in the house, and music had been blaring from the study, with the door left open: sure signs of occupation.

'Try upstairs,' she suggested.

He went past her and began to climb. 'Is it anything important?' she thought to enquire.

'Not really. He dropped his credit card in the taxi when he left this afternoon. The cabbie's a regular I often use. He handed it in.'

It sounded as though he and Oliver had spent part of the day together. So where? Not that it mattered. Margot shrugged and returned to the kitchen to dole out fruit crumble to Miranda and Charlie.

She supposed twenty minutes or so must have passed before Toby came down again trailed by Oliver with his thinning hair on end and wearing only cotton underpants and flip-flops. He saw his friend to the front door.

Curious, Margot went out into the hall to pick up their low conversation. Oliver was struggling for words. He had gone almost weepy, reaching up for the other man's shoulders and hanging on. They stood there locked together for a moment, the taller man rubbing Oliver's back as if comforting a child.

'Toby, thank you. I – I – you always make me feel... safer. You give me moments of hope.'

Margot, watching, felt a shudder of disgust. This was the last time Toby should be allowed in the house. She would make it quite clear to Oliver. This connection had to stop. She'd believed the man was dependable, a sort of minder for her husband when he was unable to cope. But under all that urbane correctness there was something horribly intimate. Toby was a pervert, and she'd not picked up on that before.

Whatever they got up to elsewhere, she was determined it shouldn't continue under her roof. In fact, she might now persuade Oliver to move out and go to live with his lover.

She sat silent over the meal while the children bickered. Miranda was in waspish mood and for once Charlie was retaliating. Over the first shock about Oliver and Toby, she realised this could be to her advantage, even provide reasonable grounds for divorce. But it must all be managed discreetly. Oliver would be as anxious to avoid hitting the headlines as she was, and therefore more ready to make her a decent settlement.

At last here was a way she could be rid of him and able to make free choices in her own life. It could be the dawn of limitless opportunity.

Tomorrow she would give her solicitor a ring and get advice on how to proceed.

Chapter Six

Barry Farrow, the lighting gaffer, was feeling rotten. For days he'd suffered these heavy sweats followed by shuddering cold, lethargy and sickness with abdominal pains. His wife had already remarked on his recent hair and weight loss, nagging him to see his GP and get some treatment to put it right. He'd explained that his assistant, Carl Winslow, wasn't fit to be left in charge if he took time off to visit the surgery. It was tight enough letting Carl go off two hours early for a dentist's appointment.

He wouldn't admit to anyone that he was scared he had something really bad. He'd always kept fit, had no illness to speak of; but his father had gone off suddenly with the big C and some of his symptoms were the same.

Just another week or so and this series would be in the can. Surely he could hold out till then? He was almost alone in the studio now, raising the last hoists and checking requirements for next day's shoot. Only the floor manager was still hanging about, rattling his car keys in his pocket.

'All right?' Barry asked.

'Fine, fine.' But Jamie was scowling. 'You don't happen to know if Jenny's left?'

'Can't say. I've been up in the grid.'

'She couldn't be locked in the ladies' or something?'

'No. Lights are off through there. If you need her I've got her mobile number.'

'So've I.' There was a touch of irritability in his answer. 'Well then, I'm off. G'night.' He made for his car.

Jamie had already been out once to make sure she wasn't sitting there waiting for him. He got in, turned on the engine to warm up while he stabbed out her number. The phone rang four times before being cut.

Out on Western Avenue, Jenny, weaving through slow traffic, silenced the mobile in her pocket. She'd be certain in future to turn it off before starting for home. She'd no intention of being picked up by an overzealous copper for careless driving.

It would be Jamie calling, damn it. She'd meant to tell him she had alternative transport, but as she left he'd been in conversation with Greg Victor, who'd finally materialised after lying low all afternoon. Also, she'd had her helmet and leathers bundled under one arm, ready to scramble into outside. That would only have delayed her, having to account for them.

Inside the space-age helmet she had hidden the new wig. There was nobody about in the car park as she'd pulled it on, shaking the long blonde hair over her shoulders. No need to look in a mirror: she knew she was unrecognisable.

No one stopped her at the security lodge. They were

only bothered about strangers coming in, not leaving. They could pick up on her new appearance in a day or two, not that she ever intended using the disguise here at work. Keep the two identities separate: that was important. She'd only gone for the wig tonight because no one was about, and she wanted the fun of wearing it.

It took an extra seven minutes covering the reverse route. Traffic was slower in the evenings; the pull of home being less, she supposed, than the frantic need not to be late for work. She respected the speed limits, beyond the acceptable three mph leeway. There were other times and places she would make the speedo spin, burning rubber up the M1 for a midnight streak.

The Kawasaki was a dream; a poem, except that the only rhyme for it would be 'chewing baccy'. That reminded her that Sammy had been short on the smack delivery this week, which could mean he'd fallen for the habit himself, and she'd need to sort him out.

She accelerated to overtake a BP fuel tanker and received a two-tone toot. In her mirror she saw the driver raise a hand. She guessed that was in salute to the blonde hair streaming below the skid lid. She grinned back invisibly under her visor. Four wheels good, she told herself; but two wheels *so* much better. She was never going to miss Jamie's sad old tan Nissan with its rubbish-tip interior.

In Notting Hill, she rode past her flat above the picture-framing shop, and took a right twice, to approach its rear in the parallel street. She was lucky in sharing a house where all manner of wood and sheet glass had to be safely stored. Duncan's lock-up shed even had space enough to run the bike in. It had meant a small rise in her rent, but was she bovvered? Business was starting to boom.

She pushed her card into the electronic lock and waited as the gates slid slowly open. Then, inside, she kicked down the stand and heaved the bike onto it. It would be safe enough in the open there until she'd grabbed a meal and was ready for the night's encounters.

Duncan Rennie had gone home some two hours back, but the lower floor still had the clean smell of fresh-sawn timber, varnish and wood glue as she walked through to the front. An inner door gave access to the stairs connecting her flat with the street door. At the top she had her key ready before she noticed the splintered woodwork round the lock.

A light push on the panels and the door swung silently open. She stood listening, her heart pounding. The intruder, whoever it was, could still be there.

She counted to twenty and there was no sound except a muffled hum of traffic from the street below and indistinct television voices from the next-door apartment.

She recognised *Coronation Street,* with a barney going on between the pub licensee and some whining female, guaranteeing its top rating with eighty per cent conflict and twenty per cent schmalz. Sadly, *All Fired Up* wasn't in the same class.

Get real, she told herself. Someone a few steps away could be listening as keenly as she was, and not mentally wittering on about television programmes. Had he heard her come in? Was he waiting behind a door, hefting an axe handle or baseball bat?

'George, bring up the shopping, will you?' she shouted, frantically inventing. Let the intruder think she wasn't alone. Give him a chance to jump out of a window.

Still there was no scurry of movement in the dark rooms ahead. She put her faith in replacing the protective helmet, eased the door more fully open with one foot and reached in for the light switch.

Across the road the stalker still watched the front of the framer's shop, stamping his feet, which threatened cramps from the cold. He tucked his hands under opposite armpits and drew in his head like an old tortoise in retreat. The hand-knitted muffler his late mother had given him three Christmases ago irritated his neck where the rash was worst, but he made no attempt to ease it.

When suddenly the lights came on in her apartment they startled him. No one had gone in by either the shop door or the blue-painted one which he'd seen her enter by on Saturday. So had she been sitting there all this time in the dark? Or was there another entrance to the building from the rear?

He waited. A few minutes passed before she appeared in silhouette against the long Edwardian window. He watched as she closed the curtains. The show, brief and teasing, left him frustrated, wanting more.

He crossed over the road to stare in at the illuminated shop window. Tastefully spot-lit, five paintings were on show: a selection of oils, watercolours and pastels with a black curtain draped as background. It was impossible to see anything beyond it.

Perhaps she had been down there behind the curtain while he waited out in the cold. It could be that she did little jobs for the shop's owner. He could imagine her, skilful with her hands, mitring frames or cutting mounts. He doubted she was related to the old man, because he'd consulted the electoral roll after he'd discovered the address, and their surnames were different. Nor was there any obvious familial resemblance, Duncan Rennie being hawk-like, Scottish-sounding and frail, while she was the very essence of English Rose.

There was so much left to learn about her. The prospect of this research filled him with warm anticipation. And for the present, he must discover if indeed there was a rear entrance to the building. It would mean walking the length of the block and turning off, to find a minor street behind. The exercise was a welcome chance to get life back into his cramped and freezing feet.

Jenny wryly surveyed the chaos her uninvited visitor had left behind. Every room showed evidence of a rapid but thorough search. Drawers and cupboards were left open, pictures removed from the walls or left wildly askew, cushions crumpled. In the bathroom the plastic side to the bath had been removed and cracked in the process. The lid was off the lavatory cistern. Her carefully made bed had been pulled to pieces. In the lounge her carpet remained roughly folded back at one corner.

It was obvious to her what the searcher had been looking for. But who had expected to find it here? In any case he'd been unlucky, drawn a blank. Yet she couldn't be sure he'd given up and wouldn't come back.

She sat on the side of her bed and debated whether to start clearing the mess or leaving it to show to Duncan the next day. The splintered woodwork of the door would need explaining, and he'd probably insist on notifying the police. The last thing she wanted was to draw their attention and have them sniffing around.

If she claimed she'd broken in herself, having forgotten her key, he'd never begin to believe her. He knew she was reliable, and that she'd simply have helped herself to the spare key he kept, as her landlord, in his cupboard in the downstairs kitchen.

Clean up, she decided. Set everything straight, and then leave Duncan a note tomorrow regretting that, unthinkingly, she must have messed up any clues to the perpetrator. Since luckily nothing was missing or damaged, the police need not be informed. She would, of course, pay for the door to be mended and repainted.

Door or doors? she asked herself. How had the intruder got into the building in the first place? She'd noticed nothing amiss at the rear, so he'd used the street door, unless he'd managed to hide away in the shop until Duncan closed it and went home.

She went downstairs and used a torch to examine the outer door. There was no damage beyond a few scratches close around the lock. No one would be likely to notice them because the nearest street lamp was at least twenty feet away and the recess threw a shadow. All the same, she was sure they were new.

So, with a picklock to hand, why hadn't the man – man or woman – used it upstairs? Perhaps breaking in forcibly there was meant to carry a message. *This is for you, personally. See what I can do. I'm capable of violence.*

Damn him, whoever he was. She would be up half the night putting things to rights and, before that, she'd more pressing affairs to attend to out at the airfield. This would have to happen on a night when she was already fatigued after a trying day at the studio, Margot having unaccountably taken two hours off at midday to go and see her solicitor. She'd probably not meant to let slip where she was bound, and the excited opinion on set was that it concerned her contract with Telehouse.

Four more times Jamie tried phoning Jenny from home, but each time he met with a blank. Finally he sent a text: *Jenny, where the hell are you? Ring me.*

He knew that somewhere he'd made a note of her landline number but it had gone infuriatingly missing. Also he'd lent his telephone directory to the guy across the landing who'd now gone out, leaving his door locked. Jamie punched the unyielding panels and his bruised fist hurt like hell.

If she was making difficulties, so could he. He wouldn't resort to Directory Enquiries. Let her rot. He squared his jaw and went out in the night to get ever so slightly drunk.

A couple of jossers playing snooker at the club took him on and he found they weren't the idiots he'd supposed them to be. He lost over fifty quid and stood more rounds than he'd ever intended. Before he fell into bed in the early hours he tried her mobile number again. *Nul points.*

Still preoccupied with her solicitor's advice, Margot had been more than ready for the end of the working day. Again in the car park she was aware of the red Fiesta leaving as she unlocked her Audi. If it hadn't been held up at traffic lights three vehicles ahead, the compulsion might not have seized her. But there he was, and here she was behind him. Yesterday he'd told her enough about himself to whet her curiosity for more. Lodging with his parents in Chesham wasn't detail enough. No harm in tailing along to see for herself the kind of road he lived in. The detour shouldn't be too far.

But it seemed he wasn't heading home. After Beaconsfield he continued east, through Gerrards Cross, to a roundabout at the start of Western Avenue.

Not in the mood for London clubbing, Margot was deciding to turn back. And then the Fiesta took a left into a dipping minor road leading, she guessed, to somewhere behind Denham Village. The unlit lane narrowed and she switched the headlights up on beam to find room to reverse.

She had lost sight of the red car among the thick vegetation ahead and was furious with herself for getting hemmed in. The ground here was soft and she was aware she might easily get stuck in the muddy tracks where other cars had tried to turn.

Concentrating on the steering, she was startled by a

tapping on her window. A face loomed palely at her and she cowered away.

'Margot, carry on another ten yards. It opens out and there's a place to park round the corner. After that, I'm afraid, it's on foot.'

But she didn't want to go on. She didn't want to be here at all. Most of all, she didn't want Nicco to know she'd been following him. But the reality was that she had done, and now he knew it. The shame of it was crushing.

Following his instructions, she recalled that yesterday he'd told her he half-owned a narrowboat on the Regent's Canal. But she'd imagine it moored somewhere upmarket like Little Venice, not down a muddy country lane in South Bucks. So could she use as an excuse that it was the canal boat she'd been eager to see? As a possible location for some video a friend intended making. It could be about bringing up children on a canal instead of in houses: a documentary called *Waterbabies*. Was he likely to believe that?

She drew up, doused the lights and unbelted. He appeared alongside and opened the door for her get out. 'What kind of shoes are you wearing?'

'My studio flatties. They'll be all right.'

She found his hand on her arm, pulling her close. Before she knew it he was hard against her, reaching for her face and tipping it towards his mouth.

Oh my God, no! she screamed inside. How could he be so sure of her? How *dare* he?

But then it didn't matter. She was engulfed.

How long they stood there clasped together she could

not guess, but she was kissing him back, devouringly, running her hands through the glossy black curls, feeling the strong angles of his face, yielding to his body. It was wonderful. And then they were walking, following a flashlight he directed ahead.

The shape of a long hulk painted in two shades of fuchsia loomed out of a light mist. He helped her climb on a high metal step that clanged like an empty water tank, and she waited while he dealt with a heavy padlock and chain. Square double doors of a hatchway slid apart; lights came on below-deck, and she was looking down into a tidy little galley with a row of five shining saucepans hanging in a row above a polished steel sink.

'Three steps down,' he warned her, steadying her arm. 'It'll warm up quickly while I put the kettle on for some tea.'

'All mod cons,' she said faintly. It was the first time she had spoken since leaving the studio. It was all amazing. She didn't have to make up any story to account for being here. There was nothing to explain. They had said it all, together. He understood perfectly. Because, sooner or later, here or some other place, he had known it would happen. Despite herself, she shuddered, uncertain quite what she felt going through her.

Still in her overcoat, she sat on a green leather sofa in a room shaped like a railway carriage, content not to explore until he was ready to show her around. Opposite, there was a heavy continental wood-burner stove ready set, and as he put a wax taper to the kindling it fired up at once.

He brought a tray with two mugs of tea and a half-full

bottle of scotch, from which he added to both. 'No cake,' he said. 'Sorry, but we don't do cake.'

'*We?*' she dared to question, then was afraid he'd think her jealous. Which – maybe – she was, already.

'Charles Jolyon,' he said. 'I told you. He's a barrister in Grays Inn. He's only here weekends. Not always then.'

'I have a son called Charlie,' she said vaguely. 'Oh, my God! The kids. I have to phone home, make sure there's someone there to look after them.'

He left her to it and came back a few minutes later in a towelling bathrobe. 'Everything taken care of?'

'Oliver's at home – my husband. I explained: something came up.'

He grinned broadly. 'It certainly did.'

She couldn't miss his meaning but pretended she did. Then a smile broke though and they were laughing in each other's arms.

Eventually, 'Won't you give me the Grand Tour?'

They started at the bows with its single bunk and computer work station, came back through the dining room-lounge and galley, with a peek into the minute heads and shower room.

They ended where a king-size bed occupied almost the whole of the stern. As in the other rooms there were sizeable square windows on either side, but these were covered with dark blinds.

'Try it,' he said, patting the bed. 'It gives quite a bounce.'

Chapter Seven

Wednesday, 19th November

Oliver Charrington replaced the receiver. He felt crushed that Margot had to stay overnight in town. The house seemed empty when she wasn't in it; not that she was ever very visible here. He wondered why the emergency meeting had been called at the company head office in London, and hoped it didn't mean the chop for a new series under her direction. Her career meant so much to her. Everything went more smoothly when she felt she was an accepted success.

She'd stayed away overnight a few days back, but he hadn't been home himself and the child-minder had grumpily stayed on. This time Margot had actually phoned him and explained that discussions could go on for hours, so she'd booked in at the small hotel round the corner. That was good. He didn't want her driving home in the early hours when she was overtired. You could lose concentration. He'd had enough of that in his time.

The children had been put to bed half an hour ago, but

he knew they had their own arrangements. He went up
to Miranda's room and found Charlie installed at the far
end of her bed with the magnetic set of Scrabble balanced
between them.

'Who's winning?' he asked. 'Shall I take over the
scoring?'

'No,' Miranda said brusquely. 'I'm doing it. Why don't
you go to bed?'

He hesitated at the door. 'Mummy's staying over in
London tonight. I thought you ought to know. If you need
anything, I mean.'

Miranda added three letters to the word *harrow*.
'*Harrowing*,' she said proudly. 'I knew that would go
somewhere if I hung on to it. That's fifteen points and a
pink square; so thirty in all.'

Clearly they didn't need anything. Certainly not him.
'Well, don't go on too long,' he said weakly. 'You've school
tomorrow.'

'Your go, silly,' Miranda reminded Charlie, who had
looked up to grin at his father. 'Can't go,' he claimed. 'Got
no vowels.'

'Well, join it on, then. Use what's already on the board,
stupid.'

Oliver closed the door on them and wandered off.
Halfway downstairs he decided to surprise Margot with
a bunch of roses, though it wasn't likely Interflora did a
24-hour service. But he could have the hotel send up
something tasty when she arrived: a half of Champagne
and some interesting sandwiches.

He remembered the hotel's name, but had to ring

enquiries for the phone number. When he was put through he asked for Mrs Margot Charrington, booked in for a single night.

It seemed she hadn't yet arrived. There was some further difficulty. The night receptionist was foreign and couldn't pick up the name at first. After a while of riffling through his register he declared flatly that there was no booking under that name.

'But that's the name she always uses.' Unlike some others with pseudonyms that were a soundbite in themselves, Margot had been pleased to use her married name professionally, and he was proud to hear her called by it. 'Look again,' he suggested. 'This would be a late booking, an emergency. Perhaps whoever took it made a note somewhere else.'

By now the receptionist was adamant and Oliver was getting short-tempered.

'Well, bloody well write it in now, and be sure you give her your best room.' He detailed the order he wanted sent up on her arrival.

It seemed that a deposit was required. He patted his pockets and produced a credit card, read off the needed information and hung up, cursing the inability of immigrants to cope with the English language. By now he felt thoroughly irritated and unready for an early bed, knowing sleep would evade him.

He had denied himself a scotch a while back out of respect for old Toby, but it was time that he showed some respect for himself. He retired to his study, turned on something bizarrely forensic on Channel 5 and settled in with the decanter.

Thursday, 20th November

Margot awoke early and knew immediately where she was. Nicco's right arm lay heavy across her ribs and was slightly sweaty. As she moved it clung to her flesh. She drew in deeply the smell of him. It was the same as the smell of the narrowboat; a mixture of wood smoke, alcohol and a musky sexiness she hadn't noticed before.

She was hungry. The pasta he'd fed her last night hadn't matched up to what she was used to. But, more than breakfast, she needed Nicco. She pushed herself away, resting on one elbow so that she could see his face in focus, and slid a finger over his lips, which were slightly pouting, cherubic. He was more than handsome. You could only describe him as beautiful. Yet masculine. She shivered. Never had she been so aware of the maleness of any man.

'Nicco,' she commanded, 'wake up!'

He gently bit her finger, opened his eyes and laughed up at her. 'I was never so awake.' His fingers started running through her hair, teased at the torn shoulder of her chiffon blouse. His lips searched for her left ear as he whispered, 'A sweet disorder in the dress/ Kindles in hearts a wantonness.../ Does more bewitch me, than when Art/ Is too precise in every part.'

When will he fail to surprise me? Margot marvelled. *Herrick?* Whoever even read his poetry today? But he'd misquoted, and it should be 'clothes', not 'hearts'.

She attempted cynicism. 'I think we've covered the wantonness already, don't you?'

'But there will be more, much more.' He looked so confident, glorying in himself and his male dominance, that she was outraged. 'What makes you think that?'

And then he was just a boy again, rebuffed, eyes fugitive, lower lip trembling as if he fought back tears. It twisted her heart. She reached for his face and smoothed back the black curls that hung about his shoulders. He was so beautiful, physically perfect, and vulnerable beyond her imagination.

'There will be other times,' she promised. 'Many, many more.' He was, she knew now, meant for her, an experience undreamt of, and this was her late awakening. For so long, wasn't it disorder she'd been lacking in this sterile, organised world she'd bound herself into? Here was her escape. Her secret lover.

'Take me,' she said, pleading, and then desperate. 'For God's sake, Nicco, don't make me wait.'

They drove separately to work. Still dark, it was the start of what must turn into a glorious day, golden and crisp with streaks of filmy white cloud sailing high: more like an intimation of coming spring than a run-up to Christmas. Margot was singing inside; something wild and joyous. In her driving mirror she watched the red Fiesta following her. Reeling him in, she thought. But in fact it was the other way round. She was the fish, helplessly netted. Yet at the same time jubilant, gloriously immune, unbeatable. She knew that today she could achieve anything she set her heart on. At work, whatever frustrations were thrown at her, she would overcome them, produce something almost flawless.

'My lover,' she told herself aloud. It was unbelievable. But so right. And – even better – she was his *mistress*.

Jenny Barnes removed her skid lid and ran a hand through her short, red hair. She sat straddling the bike while she watched Margot draw into her reserved parking space. A couple more days of walking in her shadow and then she'd be free of Telehouse for a fortnight. After that, a more exciting life as assistant to Rod Fleming, who was really keen to take her on board. Still within the same company, he had promised last night to fix her transfer to drama. And her little private project was coming along well. There'd been the break-in, of course, but it hadn't unnerved her; still might have been a coincidence: her turn for a visit from the overfriendly neighbourhood intruder. And in any case, she was wise enough to have taken precautions.

She noticed the tan Nissan parked near the studio entrance and reminded herself that Jamie would be on the warpath. She should have got him a little present as thanks and to signal a definite rupture with sharing his car. But what did you give to a man who had no interests outside work? A couple of bin bags to clear out the rubbish he chucked in the back of the Nissan? He was an odd one, so meticulous in his planning professionally and such a schmuck in his personal life. Two personas under one skin. And pretty hopeless in bed.

Nicco was just ahead of her as she went in. He turned

and grinned over his shoulder, the brilliant toothy flash he used on all women. She wondered if she'd imagined he was making a dead set for Margot at the moment, plying her coffees and lending an ear when she was in moaning mode. He'd certainly feathered his nest by upstaging Walter, his senior. He was assured now of slipping into that place on Walter's imminent retirement.

It was a dog-eat-dog life in television, pathetic the way people came and went. Even worse how some of them stayed on forever and blocked promotion. It was a good thing she'd a second string to her bow. And working alongside Fleming she could soon be milking the job for further contacts. Television was a dependency culture, and she'd found her market.

Tonight they'd be recording, with a booked audience and the raked seating slid into place. There was the usual buzz of preparation, Margot in full prima donna act up in the gallery, with Athene alongside in super-intense concentration. A weird working couple, Jenny reflected. If she stayed much longer in this job, would she end up as either? Ice Matron or a Bloated Brain?

At the steps to the gallery, Walter was taking it out of Nicco, making hay perhaps while the sun still shone in his watery sky. The younger man had flushed and his mouth was set in a single straight line. He'd been about to go up the steps for some reason when Walter called him back.

'Hell,' he muttered, and handed Jenny a silver mobile phone. 'It's Margot's. Tell her she left it behind, will you?'

'No problem.' She stared after him. Left it behind where? Had they dropped in somewhere for an early breakfast and some unofficial discussion? Surely not spent the night together? Nicco had been making a move on her, but could he have scored already? Certainly their cars had driven in at much the same time.

Jamie was heading for her, a steely gleam in his eyes. She slid the mobile into her pocket and summoned up a casual smile. 'Missed telling you last night: I've invested in my own wheels. Hope you didn't hang around waiting.'

'Nuh,' he said, after a drawn breath. 'No more than you did.'

Oliver watched the child-minder scoop the children into her car and drive off furiously. They were going to be late for school; not the woman's fault, but Charlie had taken some waking, dropping off again twice after being called at 7.45. At his age, Oliver had been like a jumping bean hours before that, even in winter. Kids today were different, easily rattled and, although scornful of their elders, crazy to be taken for adult. Funny, that.

He drifted about the ground-floor rooms, noted the good weather and debated what to do about it. If he'd had a dog...but Margot had vetoed getting one, despite Miranda's histrionic demands. And of course she was right. After the first weeks of enthusiastic care for the animal the children would have delegated its needs to everyone else. It would have been yet another useless toy left to get tatty.

His mobile started on the 'Flight of the Valkyrie'. Toby's number flashed up. 'Toby,' Oliver greeted him. 'Nice day, what?'

'For some. I'm afraid Badger's landed in UC Hospital.

It seems he fell off the platform while performing at some amateur jazz night. A broken collarbone, two ribs and one wrist. And the trumpet too, more fatally. I thought you might like to look in on him. He's not at his most cheerful.'

Oliver hesitated. 'You know what hospitals do to me.'

'If I took you along, say midday? They'll have sorted him a bit by then.'

'My car's still in dock, having the front bumper and headlights replaced.'

'There are trains…Oliver, are you still there? For an old friend, eh?'

'I was going to walk the dog.'

'You don't have one.'

'That's partly the trouble.'

'So?' Toby was so persistent. He could go on forever like this.

'Oh, all right then. I'll take a cab to the station. And another one from Marylebone.' He made it sound like a complicated manoeuvre.

'Good man. See you later then.'

The idea of Badger laid low in alien surroundings, deprived of scotch and grieving for his deceased trumpet, was anything but bracing. Oliver forced himself to shower, dress and order a taxi. In the train he was embarrassed to have the 'Valkyrie' follow him. He intended to kill the call but hit the wrong button. An obsequious male voice began an inconsequential reference to the head office of Telehouse, London.

Oliver, who abominated overhearing others' phone calls

in public places, was aware of equal irritation on the faces of travellers near him. Nevertheless, this puzzle intrigued him.

'Just a minute. Who did you say you are?'

It was the manager of the hotel Margot had stayed at overnight; a native Brit, actually speaking recognisable, suave-toned English.

'Tell me again,' Oliver pursued. 'What is this about?'

'I recognised your name,' the man claimed. 'My wife and I always used to watch your programmes. We do miss them since you retired. Well, I've a friend who works round the corner at Telehouse offices, and I happened to mention your request last night. Then he told me your wife would be at their studios down in Maidenhead.'

So far this seemed to make sense but not prime-time news. 'And?' Oliver pursued.

'I'm sorry that we had to charge for the no-show. It's company policy, I'm afraid. But as the room service was not supplied, I decided to phone in person and assure you that we had already put a cancellation for that through to your card company, and it will appear as such on their next statement to you.'

Bemused, Oliver murmured, 'Right. Thank you.' Never mind the business about the credit card company, what did the man mean by a no-show?

'It's been such a pleasure to speak with you, Mr Charrington.' The man seemed delighted to have contacted even so passé a celebrity.

'For me too.' He killed the call. Then, immediately, he knew he needed to know more. If Margot hadn't turned up as planned, what on earth had happened to her? She

102

could be injured somewhere and desperately needing his help. He tried her number but the mobile was turned off.

Calling Directory Enquiries, he was put through to Telehouse, London, and was passed from person to person until somebody could check on her attendance at last night's emergency meeting.

She hadn't been there. There'd been no meeting.

Again he dialled her mobile number. It was still switched off; which it would be, if she was at the studios by now and had started work. He would have to go there and make sure she was all right.

Decanted on the platform at Marylebone, he cursed that he'd been travelling in the contrary direction. Rather than waste time looking up cross-country trains, he'd take a cab direct to Maidenhead.

Margot's voice came through on Jenny's headset with a totally unnecessary reminder about the scene they were to work on. 'Yes, yes,' the girl said, not disguising her impatience. In her pocket Margot's mobile phone pulled at the tight fit of her stretch jeans. The old cow could wait for its return. She couldn't use it anyway until they were due a break.

For Jenny the day dragged on, much the same as before except that after the lunch break she was aware of Oliver Charrington, accompanied by a doorman, making his way towards the gallery steps. She stood, stretching stiffly, and waved to him. He broke away and came across looking worried. 'Hello, Jenny. I dropped in to see Margot. Is she all right?'

'Fine, I think. She's just getting something sorted with our producer. Can I fetch you tea or something?'

He declined and she handed him Margot's mobile. 'Maybe you'd let her have this when she comes free. Nicco handed it in. She'd left it with him somewhere.'

'Oh.' He'd not heard of any Nicco. Margot seldom confided anything about work.

'Right. Thanks, Jenny.' Absent-mindedly he switched the phone on and immediately the ring tone started up. A number on the display looked vaguely familiar. He pressed for Receive. It was Frederick Domin, of Domin, Charteris and Freebody solicitors.

'Hello,' Oliver said, 'were you wanting Margot? She's busy at the moment. Can I help?'

Domin appeared slightly flustered. 'Ah, Oliver. I wasn't expecting you. Well, actually, your wife has been in touch with my junior partner and he overlooked that we already represent you. So he can't properly take on her case.'

'Why not act for both of us? There's no conflict of interest.'

Domin hesitated, gave a dry cough. 'Well, actually, it's a little difficult. Perhaps you should have a word with her yourself, Oliver. I shouldn't really discuss the matter with you at all. It's unfortunate. I trust you are keeping well?' Hurriedly he excused himself and broke off the conversation.

Most odd, Oliver decided. He'd never known Domin even slightly rattled before. It was almost as though he imagined Margot was seeking advice about some matter that her husband was unlikely to support.

He decided belatedly that he did feel thirsty and moved towards the tea bar. He might even grab a Danish or something to fill the sudden empty void inside.

There was a movement towards him, greetings from several techs he remembered from his days at the Beeb. As the break ended he found a seat on the empty audience block and prepared to watch Margot's present production on screen.

It was only faintly amusing. Without audio access to gallery link-up, he was cut off from Margot's directions to actors and the floor manager below. Quietly he slunk outside and sat on a low stone wall at the entrance, staring at her phone, which had already disturbed him. If Margot had problems she needed legal advice on, why didn't she come to him? Worries shared were worries halved. Wasn't that it? But she was too proudly independent to ask for help.

Maybe he could do something, even without being asked. There were text messages unopened on her phone. Something among them might explain whatever it was that troubled her.

He pressed to open the first.

Chapter Eight

The first message was from a Martin Freebody. Oliver didn't recall anyone called Freebody in Television, but the name was recently familiar. Could this be the junior partner old Domin had mentioned earlier?

His text appeared to confirm this, but gave no clue to the matter that was worrying Margot. The solicitor reminded her that the subject could only be discussed further in person and confirmed the date and time she had suggested for an appointment. Apparently he'd sent the message before Domin had stepped in to apply protocol.

Unsatisfied, Oliver opened the second message. It was from the headmistress of Charlie's prep school, regretting that she had received no reply to her enquiry regarding the burns on the little boy's hands, and requesting that Mrs Charrington make an appointment to see her via the school secretary, since at present Charlie appeared to be sleepy in class and uncharacteristically out of sorts.

I should make sure he goes to bed when he's sent, Oliver thought guiltily. The boy was normally obedient, but never stood up to his sister's overbearing demands. She was the stronger character, took after Margot in that. He supposed there was a lot of himself in little Charlie.

He didn't see how Margot would ever get the time to go and be lectured by the somewhat daunting Mrs McDowell. It might take some of the stress off if he offered to step in himself, unpleasant though it would be. He recalled, a day or two back, asking Charlie about the bandaged hands, and Miranda had rushed in with some silly joke about hot potatoes. Both children had laughed and he'd left it at that. Now he'd have to find out what really happened. As for the boy being sleepy in class, maybe that had been partly his, Oliver's, fault. He'd have to admit it to the woman.

He doubted it was the headmistress's original query that had sent Margot to consult a solicitor, but the texts he'd already read were dispiriting enough to put him off opening the third. He dropped the closed phone in his pocket, rose to his feet and opted for returning to the studio floor. Immediately, he walked into Margot deep in conversation with a dark-haired young man beside camera two. She turned on him, heatedly. 'Jenny told me you were here. What's wrong?'

'Nothing. Not with me, I mean. I thought you might be unwell or something. Since I hadn't heard, I mean. I thought you'd be staying at the Gatehouse—'

'I changed my mind. Look, this next stage is crucial. I'm bloody busy and I'd rather you weren't here, Oliver. Go home.'

'I thought I'd wait and get a lift with you this evening.'

'Oh, for God's sake, take my car. I'll use someone else's. Here, take the keys.'

She dragged them from her shoulder bag.

There was so much he needed to ask her, but knew it wasn't the time or place. The young cameraman was watching the exchange with open curiosity. It made Oliver ashamed of being so spineless. He reached for the car keys. 'I'll see you later,' he said. 'There are things I need to discuss with you.'

She turned cold eyes on him. 'I could say much the same myself, but I'll be very late home and it will have to wait.'

Out in the car park he turned on the ignition and realised he had never driven this car. Margot hadn't had it long and it was her holy sepulchre. Since she was allowing him to drive it home, maybe he'd imagined she was angry with him. It would simply be pressure of the job getting to her. Later, when she was relaxed, he would offer to help with whatever was worrying her.

He drove with extra care, scrupulously keeping to the speed limits even in the absence of safety cameras.

As the run-through proceeded, Margot was having more and more trouble getting Roger into character. There were endless repeats. At one point the actor broke off to approach a boom and shout up to her, suggesting an addition to his speech. Actors were always tiresomely eager to build their parts. She breathed into her mike, 'For God's sake, Jamie, deal with him.'

A run-through was meant to be continuous. Thank God Athene was there, logging the interruptions by split seconds. Margot watched on screen as the floor manager stepped in, almost snarling, 'Roger, go back on your mark. We'll pick up from Maggie's line – "Well, that sounds a bit naughty".'

This was the big scene of build-up sympathy for the station officer's middle-aged romance. The script had turned out better than expected and the woman was good, but all she could get from Roger was tetchy offhandedness. Now, after this rebuff, he could go into deeper disgruntlement. He did, and muffed his next lines.

'Cut,' Margot called; and by mike down to Jenny, 'he's stiff as a starched plank. For God's sake, go and see what you can do with him. I'll carry on with Timmy's scene with the nursing home matron while you massage the bloody man's ego.'

Jenny collected him off the set. 'Roger,' she comforted him. 'Let's find somewhere a bit private and let our hair down, shall we?'

'That flaming Margot, I'll kill her!' he exploded. 'Do you know what Greg let drop this morning? I'm being written out. And no contract renewal. This is the last of the series for me. What the hell am I going to do?'

'Grab some fame on the strength of these last couple of days. You can do it, Roger: a great romantic moment and a tragic end. Your audiences are going to remember you for ever. There are actors who would die for the part.'

'Bloody hell, I'm going to have to!'

'It wasn't Margot's idea.'

'But she went along with it. Greg would have given in if she'd stood her ground. No, she's all for it. She as good as told me she thinks I'm shit!'

'Well, we know better. Rodge, I think I know what you need right now.'

He grasped her arm. 'Jenny, I'm skint. I'll have to owe you.'

She patted his shoulder. 'Rodge, this is a very special occasion. You're going to go out there and stun the blistering lot of them. Take it, as a gift. You deserve it. You're special. People are going to be talking about your performance as the best you ever gave.'

His eyes were desperate. 'Greg once caught me at it. Maybe that's why—'

'Nuh, he's a man of the world, Rodge. He just thought he *ought* to disapprove. While they're all busy with the Timmy scene, we've got time. And it's not that you're hung up on the stuff. You can stop any time you want to.'

'Yeah. It's just that sometimes I need—'

'—something a bit extra. For hitting the high notes. Let's trot over to the Gents. You'll have it to yourself. I'll stand guard at the door; and if anyone comes, explain you're bringing up your breakfast.'

Oliver was home in time to fetch the children from their schools; first Charlie, during which operation he kept his head well down for fear of the headmistress spying him from her window. Miranda was already impatiently waiting with a group inside her school gate, escorted by a hearty looking woman in sports gear. They were very security-conscious here ever since a nine-year-old had been whipped away by an estranged father with a restraining order served on him.

It was some time since Oliver had driven for the school run and he hoped he'd be recognised as a parent. He smiled as benignly as he felt able. Miranda marched towards him with a reassuring scowl, which screamed of familiarity. 'You've got Mum's car,' she accused him.

'Er, yes.' He opened the rear door to let her in. 'Don't forget your seatbelt.'

Miranda withered him with a glance.

'How about we stop off for some ice cream,' he suggested, hoping to mitigate her barbed indifference.

'Oh, fab,' Charlie sighed in bliss. 'I'll have a banana split with choc sauce.'

Friday, 21st November

Margot was as good as her word. It was 3.14 a.m. by the longcase clock in the hall as her taxi's headlights shone in the front windows. As she came in her eyes looked heavy, but she still glowed with a sense of achievement. Until she saw Oliver, in dressing gown and slippers, waiting for her at the kitchen door.

'How did it go in the end?' he asked.

The question seemed to wrong-foot her. 'Oh, the recording? Surprisingly well, I suppose.' She nodded. From somewhere Roger had managed to produce a slightly comic clumsiness, making him seem almost endearing. The object of his supposed affection had picked up on it and been convincingly won over.

Oliver recognised excitement in her. She was no more

ready for bed than he was. Both needed to wind down. 'You need a drink.'

She wasn't sure she did, being on a high, with the continued feel of Nicco's arms round her and his chest hard against her breasts. A faint smell of him lingered in her nostrils: something he used on his hair to make it so glossy.

She stared at Oliver and hated the thin fuzz that stuck out round his head. You could see the light through it. 'Why don't you go to bed?'

But he had told her at the studio that they needed to talk, and he plunged in now. 'Margot, I had a call from old Domin. He told me something was worrying you. Why didn't you tell me? You know I'd do anything I can to help. You've only to ask.'

Her mouth dropped open. It took a moment for her to catch her breath. *'Ask?'* she screamed it at him, resentment too long controlled breaking out as she pushed him ahead of her into the kitchen. 'You can bet your damned life I've something to ask. To *demand*. I want a divorce, Oliver. I've put up with this mock-marriage too bloody long already.'

She saw his face blanch as her own flushed with fury. 'That disgusting Toby Frobisher! How long have you two been carrying on in that filthy manner? And under my own roof, in our children's home! Don't deny it. I saw you myself.'

He was speechless, putting up protective paws like some small supplicating rodent.

'You disgust me. And he's supposed to be a *doctor*, treating you.'

'He is,' Oliver managed to get out.

'Well, I'll not have it. I want to be free of you. And you needn't imagine you've any chance of getting custody of the children. Not that you'd know how to treat them anyway. I can prove you're an unfit father.'

Oliver felt behind him for a kitchen chair and sank on its edge. Where was all this coming from? What crazy notion had she got in her head? Toby, of all sainted people! What was he supposed to have done?

'No!' he cried in anguish. 'You don't know what you're saying.'

He shut his eyes away behind his hands, to hide her engorged face, but the image stayed of her mouth opening and shutting like a fish, with all these unimaginable words tumbling out like cut-out letters from a magazine all jumbled together – the sort of thing poison pen writers made up to terrify their victims.

'No.' he moaned again.

'Bloody fucking *yes*!' she shouted and he heard the kitchen door slam behind her. Then silence.

He couldn't move for a while, but then the rocking began, backwards and forwards unceasingly, his face still hidden in his hands. Somewhere from the rooms above he heard a child's wailing start up and an angry shout to drown it out. But the protest went on, more high-pitched, broken off in a sharp cry of pain.

Charlie! Oliver thought, and it wrenched him. But he knew he couldn't go up there and put it right. He would only make things worse. There was nothing to be done. The whole world had gone mad.

Some time later he went out and stood on the back doorstep. A fine sleet had begun and he could feel its pricking chill on his scalp, through the thinning hair. The cold wrapped itself around him, dulling all else. Behind him the house was an alien place. He started moving unsteadily down the three stone steps and away along the garden path.

Margot drove off a bare four hours later after sleeping like a dead thing, waking with the alarm clock, dashing through the shower and snatching fresh clothes from the airing cupboard. There was a lot to get through before the final recording tonight, and then there'd be the studio party to celebrate another series in the bag. It would mean having to circulate for a while, receiving the congratulations, before she was free to run off to the narrowboat with her lover.

Slapping on make-up, she'd been fiercely glad that she'd made it clear to Oliver that their life together was over. He hadn't a leg to stand on. He would have to give in, because if she decided to make the situation public Toby's career would be finished. Who would want a sexual pervert meddling with their mind? God knew there were gays aplenty in the Arts, but Medicine must surely demand some degree of surface decency.

Arriving at the studio, she saw Jenny getting off that ridiculous bike and folding her leathers into the top box. Clasping her helmet under one arm like an astronaut, she started making for the entrance. Margot dropped her driving window and shouted across for her to bring her a chocolate croissant and a skinny latte up to the gallery.

Eating anywhere near the equipment was forbidden, but this was the final day and she was Margot Charrington after all. Who was likely to argue?

Her breakfast took its time coming. Athene, by then seated and ready for work, must have overheard the demand and offered, 'Stay put, Margot. I'll go and hunt it up.' As ever, she came up with the goods.

It was near 11 a.m. when a quiet tapping at the back door disturbed the cleaner mopping the kitchen tiles. She unlocked and opened it to find Oliver Charrington standing there, unshaven and shivering in his soiled dressing gown. He walked past her without any explanation, leaving a faint scent of paint and fertiliser to fight with her cleaning chemicals.

He moved stiffly, climbing the stairs and leaning heavily on the banister rail, which squeaked damply at each touch of his hand.

She would need to polish it again. He looked as if he'd spent the night in his garden shed.

She heard his bedroom door close and followed him up. With her head against the panels, she thought she heard the bed creak once. There was no sound of water drumming in the shower. He had gone to bed just as he was.

Lying on his back, staring at the ceiling, his thoughts flew to Badger in hospital, but that breezy little man had no more than broken bones and bruises. They would heal. It was remiss not to have gone to visit him with Toby. But

Toby! That was something else. He couldn't trust his mind to go there.

There was water in the carafe by his head. He poured a glassful and popped two amitryptyline in his mouth, hesitated and swallowed a third. It wouldn't make Margot's anger go away, but it might relieve his torture; for a while anyway.

His dreams were chaotic, with times and places jumbled. At one moment he was walking beside his father, who was young and in an Air Force uniform just like his Second World War photograph in the study. But he had suffered some speech defect and was desperately unable to tell Oliver something vitally important.

Without warning he was on his own again, rushing downhill on a ski slope, but in bare feet and pyjamas. Close to his chest he was clasping something alive which squirmed to get free, while a flock of black crows circled and dived at him to peck out his eyes. And then, screaming down in flames came his father's Spitfire, terrifying him awake.

And that was all wrong, because Dad had survived the war, or else Oliver would never have been born. It was his mother he had killed in childbirth, the beautiful concert singer whom he'd never had a chance to know or hear. And then, although marrying a second time, Dad had slowly, over the years, fallen apart, until the awful end.

He had never been as alone as waking now. He'd lost them all over again. Everyone had left. If he went on lying here he would feel himself slowly mortify, decay, start to smell.

Blindly he reached for yesterday's clothes and struggled into them. Out in the street he reached in a pocket. For some obscure reason the mobile was Margot's, but he could use it to ring for a taxi. While he waited for it he stood on the edge of the pavement, unaware of the cleaner watching from a front window, uncertain whether to contact his doctor or not.

Reaching the studios he found he'd no money in his pockets. He must from habit have emptied his loose change and credit cards on to the bedside table when he undressed.

The cabbie was unfazed. 'Pay me next time, Mr C,' he said confidently. 'I know you well enough by now.' But Oliver had a horror of debts. He undid his left cuff and took off his Rolex.

'Here. Will this do? For the moment?'

He knew where to go. He needed peace and quiet, to become invisible while seeing everything that went on. He had to try and swim back against the current, find himself as a part in others' lives, if he was ever to be himself again.

The raked seating was already set in place, ready for the evening's audience. Before the final scenes' recording, Margot would be working on costume run-throughs.

He would sit quietly, watching how it went.

The last run-through was completed by 4.55 p.m. Margot gave her eve-of-battle speech down on the floor and everyone dispersed to rest before the evening's big moment. Athene stayed in the gallery, looking down from the window. She saw Jenny slip into a join in the cyclorama that shrouded the outer walls, hung to prevent accidental tilt-shots of cables and stairways. She must have come out at a different point because later she was walking Roger vigorously round the empty set, propelling him by an elbow.

Was this to work off the effects of alcohol? Earlier, when he'd been close, she'd noticed no smell of drink on him. But there had been distinctly erratic levels in his acting. If he thought resorting to a hip flask at work would solve his problems, he was a long way from the truth. She'd seen people go that way before.

Everyone started flocking back for the evening's recording. At 6.45 the audience were led through from reception and filed eagerly into the seats, their voices an excited hum. The warm-up man came on and, ready to enjoy themselves, they managed to find him hilarious.

The same mixture as before, Athene reflected. Scripts and actors came and went, but the pressures up here in the gallery were always the same. To either side, the Sound Control room and the Vision Control room enclosed the central portion where Margot held sway between the vision mixer, technical coordinator and Athene herself, all glued to the monitors. The concentration required was unrelenting. But then that's what she was: unrelenting. Had she been born that way? Or maybe it was the work that set her apart, so that sometimes she felt less of a human being than a mechanical function.

In fifty minutes the caterers would be arriving and stocking up the conference room for the close-of-production party. Everyone would be celebrating in their own individual way. And a lot of them getting revoltingly pie-eyed.

'Stand by, Studio,' Margot breathed into mike. She looked and sounded as tense as a drawn bowstring. The same adrenalin charge would be coursing through them all. Jamie signalled up that the Floor was ready and at the director's order began the countdown. Athene quietly joined in. At zero minus two seconds Margot commanded, 'Go, Grams. Fade up, One.'

And the final recording began.

It was dark and almost unbearably stuffy up in the grid. Heat rose off the brightly lit set below. There was a slight smell of lubricating oil off the hoist mechanism mixed in with dry dust.

As the shooting dragged on, interspersed with recorded excerpts to keep the audience on plot, Oliver's head kept nodding forward. It was stifling up here. He struggled to get his arms, unnaturally heavy, free of his jacket and the mobile in its pocket clanged against a steel strut on the gantry alongside. Not his phone, but the one he'd had no chance to hand back to Margot.

Muzzily, he recalled there was still one message for her on it that he hadn't opened. It might help explain what was hounding her out of her mind.

He should read it now before sleep overcame him.

Chapter Nine

Friday, 21st November

In the Serious Crime's main CID office in Thames Valley, DS Beaumont and DS Zyczynski had just completed their reports on a fatal stabbing by a crowd of teenage rowdies the previous night. The interviews had been lengthy, each of the four boys arrested swearing the knife had not been his and he'd never carried one in his life. One went so far as to claim that the victim had been the one tooled up, and certainly the dead boy's prints had been found on the weapon overlaying others, since he'd tried to pull it from his chest.

'Makes you wonder,' Z mused, 'where their parents were in all this. It happened right there in their own street. They were neighbours, and kids of that age shouldn't be abroad after eleven.'

'Remind yourself of that when you're a parent yourself,' Beaumont snapped back. 'You can't keep an eye on them all the time. The curse is that these days they're born streetwise and think their parents are little short of coffin-feed.'

He logged off his computer and swept the accumulated junk on his desk into the top drawer. They both considered they were done for the night when Superintendent Yeadings walked in with a fax sheet in one hand. They hadn't known he was still in the building. He looked jaded.

'Anyone know anything about television production?' he demanded.

Beaumont grunted, aware he could be volunteering for trouble. 'I got tickets for a comedy show coupla months back, at Telehouse, Maidenhead. Took the boy along to see a recording. He was considering a media course at the time, but it put him off.'

'Why's that?'

'Too rigorous: the audience herded into raked seating and cued for reactions. It started off with a warm-up man; jokes so unfunny you'd laugh at anything after that.

'It's all done in a bare hangar of a building, but you can't watch the actors in the flesh because of masses of bulky equipment, cameramen, lighting and sound people swarming on the floor in between. You follow the action on a set of big overhead screens. There were some howlingly funny finished sequences, mostly outdoor stuff, but the bits being recorded kept stopping and starting for retakes. Disillusioning: you'd be better waiting for the finished programme to be shown at home.'

'You've gathered enough background to partner Angus on this. It so happens this is at Telehouse studios. We have a body fallen from an overhead walkway from which they suspend a lot of equipment. I'm told it would be equivalent to dropping from a third-floor balcony onto a bare concrete base.'

Beaumont rose to his feet. 'Actually, my boy could tell you more about the set-up than I can. He stayed on afterwards to chat up a redhead chick who works there. She took quite a shine to him, showed him around afterwards.'

Yeadings looked doubtful. 'You want to take him along with you? Well, he should know enough about police work not to get in the way, but it rests with Angus to OK it.'

Great, Beaumont decided. The Boss was providing him with a chance to mend fences with Stuart. He'd been grounded last week when an elderly neighbour complained of his cycling dangerously along the footpath past her house, and it rankled still. The redhead might be double the lad's age but he would fancy picking up with her again. Assistant director, she'd called herself. It sounded important enough for her to have some pull at the studios. He'd make a detour and pick Stuart up. He would still be active on a Friday night, blogging his eyeballs away on Internet.

Yeadings continued. 'The interesting thing is that our body was a visitor, with no business being up there. He was once in Beeb television at Shepherds Bush and knew a number of the people working there tonight. Anyway, falling from a height brings up the proverbial question...'

'Did he fall or was he pushed?' both sergeants completed.

Beaumont had spoken of rigorous organisation. He hadn't been wrong. Obviously television was labour intensive, and DCI Angus Mott's first impression was that this crowd knew exactly what they were meant to be doing and were frustrated at the police presence throwing an oversize spanner in the works. Not that the incident hadn't upset them. Everyone stood or sat about in uneasy silence as the CID team entered and took over.

The young woman allocated to take him around was a redhead, lean and boyish in stretch jeans. She would be the 'chick' Beaumont's teenage son had spoken of on the way in. He'd written her name down as Jenny Barnes, assistant director, and with an address in Notting Hill, London. He'd picked up already that in general the producer's team saw to the initial planning, costing, casting and financial details, while the directors were concerned with how the film was actually made.

Mott glanced across towards the free area where Beaumont and four uniformed officers had the entire personnel sorted into groups according to function. He would have a word with him later about bringing his son along, wrongly assuming his DCI would permit it. Now the boy was confined in the car out of harm's way and probably smouldering with resentment.

Telehouse Security had taken over immediately the incident happened, and no one had been allowed to enter or leave the complex since then.

'What have you done with the audience?' Mott asked Jenny suspiciously. 'Were they sent home?'

'They'd already left, thank God. The show was over and the studio floor was almost deserted. Anyone remotely involved in the series had turned up, to enjoy the party in the conference room along the corridor. That's where most of us were when it happened. Tonight's was the final recording for this series. From then on it's just editing and the sound dub. We've nothing booked here until the autumn, after the sequel's been cast and rehearsed in a hired village hall. Studio time's too expensive for the early stages.'

Mott stared upwards. The grid might be an area for suspending lighting, but it was pitch dark now. Scenes of Crime officers would soon be swarming all over it with their own lights. The powered hoists used to lower the equipment had not yet been used. Access by stairway was already sealed off with police tape, and the heavy drapes that covered all the walls were looped up at their openings.

'Cyclorama,' Jenny said, following the direction of his eyes. 'That's the name for the all-round masking. It hides the walls and cables so that a tilting camera can't pick up anything to wreck the illusion. We call it the cyc. It only runs up to the level of the gallery floor, which is our Control room. Above that there's the continuation of staircases leading to the grid, where the lights hang. That has to be where he fell from.'

On the concrete floor a brownish area of dried blood extended beyond where the body was now covered with a canvas sheet. With death confirmed, it was about to be bagged and removed, the scene already photographed from all angles by SOCO, and measurements recorded. They were meticulous. If they said the body had fallen from the grid, then that was exactly what had happened.

'Where would you have been when he went up there?'

'Probably on the studio floor, concentrating like mad

on my monitor. You learn to cut out any distractions. I'd have felt it if everyone had suddenly disappeared, but not a single person walking behind me. You might have better luck asking the camera or sound men. They get a sort of sixth sense for things moving out back.'

'So why would anyone go up in the grid?'

She considered this. 'The only people with a real need to check up there would be the technical guys. But during recording it's out of bounds for safety reasons. Everyone's busy down at set level. There are walkways up there to access the hoist cradles. It would be total darkness in the grid at the time it happened.'

'Have you ever been up on the walkways yourself?'

'No, it's no business of mine.'

Obviously the next thing was to speak with someone whose business it was.

'Carl Winslow, he's stand-in for the lighting supervisor who's on sick leave,' Jenny told him. 'You'll have your time cut out to get a word out of him. Carl's a bit of a mute. He's gone across to the tea bar with his crew. I'll take you there.'

They were accosted on the way by a tall, loose-limbed man in frayed jeans and cowboy boots. 'I'm Jamie Graham, floor manager,' he explained. 'So I don't belong in any of the crews. Maybe I could explain who everybody is, and Jenny can rejoin the director.'

His eyes were an unusually pale blue and his straw-coloured hair stuck out like a badly assembled corn dolly.

Not as disorganised as he looked, Mott suspected. Maybe a control freak, and noticeably possessive about the girl. Or was he scared she might talk out of turn to the police? That was something to follow up later. For the moment he'd ride along with what this Jamie suggested; see where it led him.

'Thank you, Jenny,' he said. 'You've been most helpful.' He didn't miss the look of resentment darted at the man as she turned away.

'I want a word with Carl Winslow,' Mott told Jamie. 'And after that I want to question you.'

Ordered off, the floor manager stood firm a moment, challenging him; then shrugged. 'You won't get much out of Carl. He uses words like a miser gives to charity.'

It had fallen to DS Rosemary Zyczynski to interview the director's team. She wondered if Mott had decided this because all four were women. A further four were included: lighting supervisor and vision supervisor, sound supervisor and deputy sound supervisor, all of whom were men and completed the gallery control personnel.

She assumed that they, if anyone, would have been situated high enough to command a sight of everything going on below.

'Except,' the production assistant stipulated, 'that we all sit facing away from the window, concentrating on our bank of monitors or the mixer. All we see and hear is what actually goes on screen.'

She was the only one who seemed willing to volunteer information. Zyczynski looked through a list the uniform constable had provided and matched up her identity tag with her function. Her name was Athene. She was a compact woman in her late thirties with a square face, squarish spectacles and a severe expression, perhaps more concerned than actually shocked.

'Did you know the deceased?'

'Of course. Everyone in television knew Oliver Charrington; most of the adult viewing public too. As a prime time documentary presenter he'd been a household name.'

Zyczynski noted the past tense. 'He had retired?'

'He had given up, yes.'

'He burnt out,' said another woman flatly. Like the others, she wore the tag the constable had given her: Margot Charrington. This was the director, the widow. She should not have been exposed like this to group questioning.

'I'm so sorry, Mrs Charrington, for your loss: a terrible shock. Is there somewhere quiet you can go and rest?'

Margot slightly lifted her shoulders. 'These are the people I work with. I belong with them.'

Embarrassment kept the others from looking at her directly.

'I'll speak with you first,' Zyczynski said, 'and then you'll be free to go home. Is there someone who will go with you?'

The others drifted off. She confined her questions to whether Margot had seen her husband at the studio.

'No, and nobody mentioned that he was here. In fact, I hadn't seen him since I got home late last night. I left early this morning before he was up.'

'Were you expecting him to come here?'

'No. He had no reason to.'

'But tonight was to be the party.'

'He wasn't one for partying.' The woman paused as if weighing whether to add more. 'Actually, he did turn up about midday yesterday without warning, and I sent him home. He didn't appear very well.'

'In what way, Mrs Charrington?'

She looked grim. 'Oliver suffered from clinical depression. He'd been receiving therapy for years.'

That must surely be enough pressure on her for now. One of the team could visit her tomorrow at home, if Mott considered it necessary. The case would probably be logged as a likely suicide, given the history of depression.

The DS waved a woman constable across and instructed her to find a friend who would accompany Margot home.

One of the uniform men was quite a draftsman. He had drawn a ground plan of the studio, its access doors and the corridor leading to where the party was being held. Now the main concern was to plot on it exactly where everyone – actors, techs and production – had been at the time the body fell. It was significant that nobody had admitted being in the grid and nobody had actually seen it happen. Most of the forty-odd involved had already moved on to the party, and crowded back when the news reached them. There was a lot of good food going to waste now, as appetites had unsurprisingly disappeared.

'It was the sound,' the producer said. 'God, I'll never get it out of my head. A sort of heavy crunch. There was no cry, no warning. And suddenly, there he was on the floor.

We'd no idea who it was until we went across to look. I didn't know Oliver was in the building. Security on the gate must have recognised him as our director's husband and let him in without a pass.'

'As they did yesterday,' said Jamie. 'But he'd have got in under his own power, being a celebrity. He was big in television before anyone had heard of Margot.'

There was an edge to his voice. Beaumont noted that the director was not the floor manager's favourite person.

DCI Mott had been working through the lighting and Sound crews who, as action stopped, had craftily stowed their gear and reached the front row at the bar. Once their claims to have been there when the fall occurred were cross-checked he saw no reason why they shouldn't be released.

He became aware of a small woman, mid-thirties, watching him closely. Her label described her as production assistant. 'You're thinking someone else might have been involved?' she asked intently.

'We're assuming nothing, but it pays to consider every possibility. Did you know the dead man?'

'Oliver? Yes, for a number of years. We worked together on his last programme for the BBC. As a presenter he was impressive; a sensitive man, modest; before the present fashion for more brash personalities. He had a gentle sense of humour and some quite inspired ideas, drawing top ratings for subjects the general public hadn't been expected to enthuse over.'

'But he gave up television?'

'He had a breakdown a month or two after his father

died. He became reclusive, stayed at home to look after the children when they were tiny. By then Margot had moved on and become the breadwinner.'

'Became a house-husband? How long ago would that have been?'

'Six or seven years. I used to keep in touch at first, but it somehow tailed off. I regret it now. I should have made more effort.'

A quiet, thoughtful woman, Mott guessed. Would her continued friendship have kept Oliver Charrington from self-destruction? If, he reminded himself, this really was a case of suicide.

Chapter Ten

Stuart Beaumont cursed being left in his father's car opposite the windows of the Telehouse Security Lodge. One of the guards working at a computer there kept looking across to check he wasn't exhibiting the sort of villainy he obviously expected from hormone-driven young males.

Like I might try and knife somebody, Stuart thought, or smash a few windows for fun. If I get left here much longer I might well do something of the sort.

What a bloody waste of time, when Dad promised me a gory stiff.

It wasn't even as if there was a stock of cool CDs to make waiting worthwhile. He shoved back his seat and planted his trainers on the shell of the airbag. This veto was Angus Mott's doing. Since his stint in Kosovo you'd think he'd been trained in a Nazi prison camp. Angus used to be cool, a tough water polo forward with a great sense of fun.

There was nothing to see out here. The only incident of note had been when a closed black van backed up to the main entrance for a stretcher to be brought out and loaded. The body was covered, on its way to the mortuary. The guard at the lodge window came out and oversaw it driven through the powered security gates. He stood looking after it, jingling keys in his uniform pocket, turned to stare at Beaumont's car with the teenager in it, and then went back to his work.

Stuart closed his eyes and concentrated on recalling the face of the redhead who'd once given him a tour of the studios. It didn't come back as clearly as the shape of her; boyish, slim, with slightly up-tilted breasts and a tiny waist. She'd walked away with the hint of a wiggle: cheeky. Well, that's what rumps were, of course – cheeks.

He'd half drifted off when he heard raised voices coming from a side exit of the studios. Male and female – more than just arguing: ranting at each other like a Punch and Judy show. He wound down his steamed window and saw them for an instant as they passed under a security light, the man really tall and the woman barely up to his shoulder. He seemed to have her in an arm-lock and was propelling her towards the car park. After they passed into shadow he heard a single muffled shriek.

The guard at the window didn't look up from his computer. Cloth ears, Stuart thought scornfully. Well, it wasn't his business to alert him. He guessed there was a lot of rough slap-and-tickle went on among the people who worked at a place like this. Rampant sex, the lucky beggars.

Three other figures appeared at the same lighted door and stood there talking. Then slowly a stream of

134

others followed, staying in a close group in low-voiced conversation before breaking up and dispersing toward their cars. It looked as though the preliminary questioning might be almost over. CID would soon be free to depart, leaving the Scenes of Crime experts to do whatever was needed to search for clues. He hadn't expected it to break up so soon. Apparently it had been rated an accident, rather than anything more exciting: a disappointment after the rush of adrenalin a possible murder scene had promised.

From the main entrance, DCI Mott and Stuart's father emerged accompanied by a uniform sergeant and a tall civilian in a suit. As they stood in discussion, DS Zyczynski joined them. By now a steady stream of men and women in more casual gear was pouring from the side door.

Again the security guard operated the gates from inside the lodge and came out as a score of cars manoeuvred out of their designated parking spaces. As they left he saluted some, nodded to others, ignored the rest. Hierarchical society, Stuart noted cynically.

Beaumont materialised on the opposite side of the car and thumped on the roof. Stuart released the lock and he climbed in. 'Thank God it's Friday, or almost *was*. What a hell of a week. Lucky old Z, she's off to France with Max for the weekend, Christmas shopping.'

'So what's with the verdict?'

'Accident or suicide, most likely. We'll know more when Littlejohn's looked at the body. No fresh smell of alcohol on his breath.'

'Who was he?'

'A chap called Charrington. Used to work in television, but he was just visiting today.'

'Not *Oliver* Charrington? God, Dad, even you must have heard of him. He did some really cool stuff. They still do repeats on all the channels.'

'I don't have time for the gogglebox,' Beaumont said scornfully, 'but the name did sound vaguely familiar. Seems he suffered from depression.'

Stuart sighed self-pityingly. 'There's a lot of it about.'

At home, Beaumont typed up his notes on his laptop and sent them through to CID HQ, where DC Silver was correlating all received info on the incident. Saturday dawned bright and frosty. Beaumont escaped from the house to pick up wood preservative from the DIY store and two new brushes because the others had gone too stiff to waste time on cleaning them. With any luck he'd get most of the teak garden furniture covered in a first coat this weekend before the weather switched and the drizzle came back. Stuart did his teenage thing, not putting in a yawning presence until lunch was already cooling on the table. 'Where in France has Z gone shopping?' he demanded, hoping it might spark the offer to do likewise, plus a special pocket-money increment for the occasion.

'Calais and Lille. They hold special Christmas markets.' Beaumont hadn't a lot of time for Christmas in general or the need to spend money on frippery. He'd almost boycotted the season since an American family had moved in next-door two years back. They did the thing in style, with galloping reindeer and flashing Santa's sledge romping across the front lawn. Already this year a workman had been seen up on the chimney fixing some kind of decorative frame with light bulbs all over it. Doubtless there'd be an all-night party soon to celebrate switching it on. Not to mention rubber-neckers collecting in the road to gawk.

At 2.56 p.m. DCI Mott rang through. The DS was to pick up a woman constable from Area and call to question the Charrington widow discreetly for background on her husband's medical history. Someone had said that Oliver's therapist was a family friend, so find out who he was. Once he'd supplied evidence of bi-polar disorder for the coroner they could probably drop the police interest. Professor Littlejohn had so far given only a passing glance at the body, but hadn't picked up anything significant that could involve a third party.

The call caught Beaumont rolling up his sleeves to sand down the garden table. Now he had to get out of scruff order and find a clean shirt. Waste of a fine afternoon. In a far from amiable mood he collected PC Molly Strachan, a buxom fifty-year-old with a motherly manner. He was further miffed on reaching the dead man's address to discover the widow was not available for questioning.

The woman in charge there was equally put out. Carlotta Gilbey, the missing woman's mother, was a pain in the butt, addressing him as from a great height and clearly upset at the family being dragged into media attention by a son-in-law she'd had scant sympathy for. She had already frozen off a small army of paparazzi representing newspapers keen to update and amplify obituary notes prepared back in the days when Oliver had been a celebrity.

'So where is Mrs Charrington?' Beaumont demanded. 'This is the address she supplied to the police.'

'She is staying with friends,' Carlotta told him coldly, 'to avoid invasion of her privacy. I am sure she will get in touch with you when she feels able to talk to you further.'

'Do you know where she's staying?' he pressed. 'Or how long she'll be away? Did she take much luggage with her?'

Admitting she wasn't fully cognisant of the situation clearly irked the woman, but she was obliged to explain that Margot had not returned from the studios, having rung her at home late the previous night demanding she step in to relieve the child-minder, who didn't work weekends. She had baldly announced Oliver's unexpected death, probably at his own hand, and had rung off without mentioning who the friends were with whom she was staying. Since then her mobile phone had remained switched off.

'Grief can take people in different ways,' murmured the policewoman kindly.

Beaumont thought Mrs Gilbey was going to shout her down, but she managed to master her anger. 'Interesting reactions all round,' he muttered as they regained the car. 'Not a lot of sympathy shown for the poor devil from either woman.'

'On the surface.' PC Strachan attempted to moderate his bile.

As Beaumont started the car he glanced up at the elegant house front and saw two small faces at an upstairs window staring wanly down. They'd be the kids Oliver

Charrington had once retired from television to look after. Now they were older, of school age. What were they likely to feel at losing their father? He wished he'd been able to meet them and judge for himself.

It wasn't that Superintendent Yeadings had any premonitions about the Charrington death; more that when a case concerned someone the media were likely to make a fuss about, you couldn't be too careful. For this reason, he told himself, he had chosen to go in on a Saturday and run through the reports on the Telehouse fatality.

With such a number questioned, it was ironic that there hadn't been a single eyewitness to the man's fall. Perhaps he had chosen his moment for that reason. No one would ever know exactly what was in his mind at the time. Had he intended suicide when he entered the studios?

The grid was a long way up. Why had he decided to climb so far when he could have watched the whole programme comfortably from a seat in the auditorium? Perhaps because it was not this excerpt of *All Fired Up* that interested him, but someone engaged in the recording below.

Somehow he had managed to secrete himself up there in the dark without anyone being aware of his presence. More and more it seemed that it had been his intention simply to hide away until a final moment of self-destruction.

But why choose that method to kill himself? As a depressive – which was how two people interviewed had described him – he'd have had access to strong medication.

(Something like lithium carbonate or diazepam? But fashions in medicine kept changing when the side effects were studied. He'd have to bone up on the subject.)

Whatever the treatment, Oliver could have saved enough doses up until he had a potentially fatal one, to go out quietly. He also owned a car and could surely have got hold of the necessary rubber tubing to ensure a more peaceful end.

The way he'd chosen was spectacular, but enacted at a moment of minimum notice. Athene, who seemed to appreciate the man, had described him as gentle; but he'd left a horrifying corpse to be discovered after the deed. Was that to shock as many as possible in this television world he'd once abandoned? Or was it a protest aimed at one specific person? There was often a degree of revenge in the taking of one's own life.

To start with he'd wanted seclusion; at the end ostentation. Was such a swing merely symptomatic of his erratic mental state, or had something occurred in between to change his behaviour totally? If so, was the catalyst an incident he'd observed from his high vantage point, or something disturbing about the show he was watching? According to Beaumont it was light entertainment, not high drama or anything soul-searing.

Facing this sea of reports, Yeadings was dissatisfied. He needed to know the man's mind. Most of the comments recorded from those who had known him were about Charrington's outstanding work. His wife's only contribution was to call in doubt his mental stability, but the production assistant, Athene, had spoken warmly of him as a gifted and likeable person. Before he could pass a police statement to the coroner and hope to drop this inquiry, he would need to talk with her, as well as the therapist in charge of the man's treatment.

DC Silver had had everything entered into the central computer. Yeadings, still a pen-and-paper user by preference, had to admit that IT had its uses. He logged on to his laptop and copied the whole lot through for quiet perusal at home.

Home, yes. That's where he should be right now, planning a Saturday afternoon treat for the kids and giving Nan some free time. Be a good dad, like Oliver Charrington had tried to be; another man blessed with young children later in life than most.

She shouldn't have come here. Cooped up in the confines of the narrowboat with only Nicco to work out her anguish on, Margot felt the need to break out and go madly active: rush about; shout; scream; tear at her hair. How could Oliver have done this to her? It was vicious, detestable, so disgustingly physical.

Newspapers would be full of it, recalling his successes, implying all sorts of things about his family life, his relationship with her. Blaming her, even, saying that he must have been unhappy. It wasn't her fault that his talent had burnt out and he'd become a mental wreck, while she laboured to hold the family together, tried to make a name for herself. And *succeeded*. But now they'd start comparing her work with his, slightingly, which was unfair, because she had never been offered the status programmes he'd enjoyed. Life was more competitive by the time she'd started out. Oliver had peaked when it was easy to get to the top and meet little competition to prevent his staying there.

Nicco shuffled towards her balancing a full mug of coffee. Caffeine was the last thing she needed now. She was wired with a million volts.

She looked with distaste round the lounge shaped like a railway carriage but permanently stationary, never going anywhere. She felt trapped in it.

'Maybe you'd feel better at home,' he offered awkwardly.

Did he want rid of her? How could she go home? Her mother was there. Carlotta would rush to remind her she'd never liked the man; had advised her not to marry him. She would blame the scandal on her. It wouldn't help. In fact, who could? She realised she had no real friends. She had been too concerned with her work to bother cultivating any.

Nicco, who had seemed to open a whole, pulsating new dimension in her life, was useless, lacking maturity and strength. All he could offer now was sex, and the mere notion disgusted her. He was so shallow. When she discovered her phone had gone missing he sulked and swore he'd sent it back to her through Jenny after he'd found it. But actually he would have hidden it. Maybe he wanted everyone to think she'd run away, overcome at Oliver's stupid suicide. That would have created more scandal for the press to salivate over, and God knows what the police would have made of it. She'd demanded he lend her his mobile, and at least now her mother would be able to explain she was staying with friends, if anyone came asking.

She looked at him, slight, uncertain, pouting like a frustrated child. He was incapable of understanding how she was shamed by what had happened. He was only thinking about his own needs, at first vicariously excited by being in the centre of another's drama, and now scared that he would attract some of the blame.

She snatched the mug by its handle and flung the scalding coffee in his face. He screamed. It was like one of the noises peacocks make, but much louder. And that's all he was, a sexually motivated display-bird.

She should have run for it, because once he'd reached out and blindly wiped his face dry on the end of a curtain, he lunged for her, shook her by the shoulders until she saw bright explosions of white light behind her closed eyelids. Then he flung her down on the sofa, fell heavily on top and started tearing at her clothes.

Barely conscious, she endured him raping her.

Chapter Eleven

Sunday had begun in the normal manner for the Beaumonts. Audrey had recently taken to attending church at 10 a.m. for the family service, awkwardly conscious that she sat as a loner amongst the mums, dads and noisy toddlers. Teenagers were well represented as well, providing amplified and enthusiastic pop tunes for the new style hymns. She had tried to persuade Stuart there was a place for him here with his acoustic guitar, but he was scornful, needing all morning in bed to recover from the mega-surfing of the night before.

She arrived home to find that her husband was out, having turned up the heating instead of leaving opened windows to air the house the way she liked. Every room seemed to smell of yesterday's cooking and male overnight sweating.

As she heated fat for the roast potatoes and slammed a leg of lamb in her secondary oven, she rehearsed again her doubts about returning after her flight from the marital home. Her attempt to create a life of her own had fallen flat and she'd come creeping back, hoping things might return to how they'd been, but almost two years later she was still out in the cold.

Now, on top of the normal hazards of a police wife and coping with the mood swings of an intelligent and hormonal teenage son, she saw herself as an ex-lag on parole, constantly required to give proof of reform. While initially relieved at being allocated the guest bedroom, she found drawbacks in having an electric blanket as her sole source of comfort. On a few isolated occasions her husband had breached the divide, but always on the following day the coolness between them had resumed. It was probable he sometimes found substitutes elsewhere.

She sternly reminded herself that at least now she was assured of a roof over her head and the means to eat regularly while her part-time catering interest provided pocket money. If ever there was a next time she would have amassed some savings to tide her over while seeking a full-time job. She rinsed her hands under the tap and went to lay the table.

They were to gather round their Sunday lunch at 1.15 p.m., but her husband was still missing. She had a vague memory of hearing the front door slam shut at some unearthly hour. Police business, perhaps.

As she laid down the steel after sharpening the carving knife, the hall phone rang. 'That'll be f'me,' Stuart said confidently and went to take the call.

He returned grinning. 'Dad's got another body. That's pretty good going. Two in three days. I'll bike out there and take a look, and take something with me to eat.'

So that, Audrey thought, is the end of the one meal in the week when we sit down together and behave like a proper family. Just me on my own.

With the comforting pressure of a slightly warm lamb-and-mint club sandwich in the breast pocket of his anorak, Stuart cycled towards Fulmer off the A40. Deprived of Friday's cadaver, he was cheered by the prospect of an even more spectacular one. He passed through the S-bend dip of the village, where a small crowd had spilt from the pub to puff legitimately at cigarettes in the freezing cold, and turned off right towards Stoke Poges. Nothing dramatic was supposed to happen out there. It was Dullsville. All he could recall of note was a dreary graveyard poem about the Knoll of Parting Day. His empty stomach rumbled as he craned to look for the police incident tape.

Ahead, the white equipment van, two patrol cars and DI Salmon's grey Vauxhall were lined along the grass verge, but not his father's red Toyota. The burnt-out wreck he sought was half hidden among winter-bare silver birches. He remembered then that the place was infamous for prolonged heath blazes in the summer. One advantage of the frost must have been to keep these flames confined. Even then, the closest trees looked shrivelled and blackened. Whoever had set light to the car had been no miser with the fuel.

Stuart stood distantly pondering over the wreck until one of the patrol men recognised him and waved him across. 'Not one of your efforts, I trust?'

The boy snorted. 'Where's the body then?'

'Bagged and removed. Your dad's gone to follow it up.'

This was disappointing. 'So whose car is it?'

'Your guess is as good as mine. We've yet to find a readable licence plate.'

'Could the body have been in the boot before kids nicked it?'

'Anything's possible at this stage, but we've a nasty feeling about this one. It could get complicated.'

Stuart grunted. Two violent deaths to investigate in almost as many days was going to keep his dad busy, so it was just as well the business down at Maidenhead was shaping up as a straightforward suicide.

'This is a crime scene, not a public spectacle,' said a sour voice behind him. DI Salmon, of course.

Stuart cast a weather eye at the sky. It was fast clouding over. 'You'll have to look shifty removing the car. It's gonna rain buckets. You could all get bogged down,' he told him with relish.

He returned to his bike and stood there straddling it while he unwrapped and wolfed down his sandwich. 'Public road,' he reminded the DI between swallows. Salmon turned on his heel and went back to his car.

At Monday morning's debriefing Beaumont had to admit that the licence plate was still missing. 'Could have been deliberately removed,' he gave as his opinion.

'To delay identification of the car's owner,' Yeadings agreed. 'But now SOCO will be checking on the engine and chassis numbers.'

'If we knew where it had been left parked, that could

give a lead to who stole it,' DI Salmon concluded. 'Though maybe it wasn't stolen at all, and the owner's the one responsible for the body. Are there any new reports of a local missing woman who fits the age group?'

'Two women went missing in the three counties over the weekend,' Mott told them. 'A Winnersh teenager runaway, and an Alzheimer patient of seventy-three who's already been found wandering in Langley Park. Both are being dealt with by Area teams.

'I've arranged with the PR office to call a press meeting at 10.45 and I'll attend it with DI Salmon. We want the widest publicity on this crime. Meanwhile, DC Silver is working on a list of possible Audi owners in Thames Valley. It's a quality make, and fortunately there won't be so many soft tops.'

'And the post-mortem?' Yeadings enquired.

'Prof Littlejohn will do it at Wexham Park Hospital at 3.15 this afternoon. Beaumont, I want you there together with the PCs from the patrol car first called to the incident.

'Zyczynski, welcome back. This is your chance to catch up. Go and take a look at the car now it's under cover, then visit the crash scene. A constable's still on guard to keep the curious from trampling the ground, and we'll hope the rain has left it fairly intact. Now, any questions anyone?'

'I'd intended getting further background on Oliver Charrington this morning,' Z said. 'His widow should be back home by now. Is that all right?'

'Check on the torched car first. The other business

can wait. If the Prof has time to do an encore with Charrington's body after the charred one you can attend that. Contact his secretary for details.'

Back in the CID office two small packets wrapped in gift paper were on Beaumont's and Salmon's desks. The DS picked his up and sniffed at it. 'Pretty ripe, isn't it?'

'You should smell Angus's,' Z said, grinning. 'He likes his cheeses strong.'

DI Salmon looked doubtful. 'I'm not sure the wife will go for French cheese. She only buys mild Cheddar. But thanks, anyway.'

The two sergeants' eyes met. For once Salmon had sounded almost pleasant.

Zyczynski drove out to view the burnt-out scene. A desultory sleet was turning to drizzle. The uniform man left on guard was reluctant to quit his car and walk round the crime scene with her. There would be photographs enough taken by the experts, but Z had brought her digital camera to make her own collection.

Considerable tramping round the car by fire crew and police had destroyed any useful tracks, but she made a further wide search of the area to satisfy herself that the licence plate hadn't been buried somewhere or thrown up in a tree.

There was an alternative possibility. If underage joyriders had been involved, they would likely have borne the plate off as a trophy. By now it could be proudly displayed on a shelf in some teenager's bedroom. Z wrote up her report in the car before setting off for Beaconsfield and her inquiry into Friday night's suicide.

A stranger opened the Charrington's front door to Z's knock. She was thirty-ish, sharp-featured, flushed, and determined to repel all boarders. Z smiled, held out her ID and asked to see Margot.

'She's not here,' the woman told her shortly. 'It's the ruddy limit. Her mother's supposed to be covering for her, but she rang for me to come in because Miranda's being a right madam and refused to go to school this morning.'

'Is she ill?'

'No. She's faking it. I think she heard her granny talking on the phone to a friend and overheard about her father. She seems to be taking it as a personal insult. She can have a really nasty temper.'

'I think I'd be upset, in her place. Hadn't anyone told the children?'

'No, Mrs Gilbey was waiting for their mother to get back.'

'What about the other one – a little boy, isn't it?'

'Charlie? I dropped him off at his school. He seemed stunned. Miranda must have told him, but he hadn't properly taken it in.'

'So can I speak to the granny?'

'No. She had a hairdressing appointment. Won't be back until five.'

Zyczynski looked at her sympathetically. 'It's been quite a shock for you too. Have you worked long for the family?'

The woman seemed to relax. 'Five years,' she said. 'I took

over from the nanny when Charlie was two. Look, why don't you come in? I was just going to put the kettle on.'

They settled in the kitchen, a vast room of calico-coloured walls and cupboards, chrome fittings and pale green marble counters. 'My name's Joanna,' the woman told her.

'I'm Rosemary.' Gently, Z eased round to the subject of the dead man. She learnt that Joanna had liked him.

'He was no bother, always nice to people, a real gentleman, though he used to get very down at times. That was his trouble; excited one moment and then losing his self-confidence, feeling everything was wrong with himself. You'd never think he was once such a celebrity.'

'Like his wife is now.'

'Yes, well...' There seemed some doubt there. Perhaps Margot wasn't her favourite person, but she'd sense enough not to slag her off. That's where her wages came from, after all.

'But he must have had friends of his own – people from when he was in television?'

'I wouldn't know. He used to meet friends up in town. London, I mean. They were all keen on music; used to tour the clubs that had live groups playing. He'd got a lot recorded too, and when he was on his own he'd sit for hours just listening.'

That sounded lonely. 'So if I wanted to talk about him with one of his friends – one who'd known him for a long time – who should I ask?'

'Dr Frobisher, I guess. He was the closest, and used to visit here most. Oliver once said they were at school together. There's another man who plays a trumpet. They call him Badger, but I wouldn't know what his real name is or where he comes from.'

'This Dr Frobisher, what's he a doctor of?'

'He's some kind of psychologist, I think. He works at the neurological institute in Holland Park. His phone number's in the book on the hall table. I had to ring him once when Oliver had a panic attack. He dropped everything and drove straight down.'

'That sounds like the right kind of friend.' Z lifted the mug of coffee Joanna pushed towards her. 'No sweetener, thanks. Do you think he might have been afraid Oliver would end the way he did?'

Joanna frowned. 'Suicide? That's awful. You never think someone you see almost every day is going to do a thing like that, however miserable they get at times.'

'Don't you believe that's what happened, then?'

'Maybe an accident. If he went dizzy, couldn't he just have toppled over?'

'There are waist-high guard rails to prevent that. But, maybe, if he was leaning over to see something just underneath – I don't know. It's not my business to say. There has to be an inquest, and the coroner will examine where it happened.'

Z darted a glance at the other woman. She was looking distressed. 'You don't think someone else might have been up there with him, and gave him a sudden push?'

'Oh, not Oliver!' Joanna gasped. 'Who would ever want to hurt him?'

Z let the question remain hypothetical. She was

watching fleeting emotions cross Joanna's face. 'No,' she denied again. 'And, anyway, she wouldn't need to. She was going to divorce him in any case.'

But the woman was scared. Z leant across and grasped her wrist. 'You mean Margot? It's all right, Joanna. We know she wasn't up there with him. She was in the gallery talking to the vision mixer. You are probably right and Oliver just fell.'

The CID office was empty, except for DC Silver snatching a late lunch break at his desk with a spicy pizza. Z looked into DCI Mott's next-door office. Empty, too. Of course, he'd not be back until after the post-mortem on the burnt victim. That could take hours. She doubted Littlejohn would get round to examining Oliver Charrington's body today.

There was plenty in her conversation with Joanna to fill a report sheet, but she needed a sounding-board right now before she wrote anything down. And that's what the Boss had once offered to be.

She ran upstairs and found Superintendent Yeadings's door ajar. 'Come in, Z,' he said without looking up and before she could knock. Typical, she thought. I bet he knows us all by our way of walking.

'So what have you found out?' he asked, clearing aside a sheaf of papers on his desk. 'I'd offer you coffee, but the filters have run out.'

'Thank you, but I'm fine. I could go down and get you a new box.'

'I'd rather you stayed and gave me your news. Did you pick up anything out at Fulmer?'

'No. So I went on to the Charringtons' and spoke with the child-minder-cum-housekeeper. Apart from the nine-year-old daughter, there was nobody else there.' She gave him a précis of their conversation.

Yeadings listened intently until she had finished. 'So you gathered that relations between the parents were cool, if not hostile? And, if sides were to be taken, this Joanna would have been rooting for the husband?'

'Yes. She obviously feels some sympathy for him. He sounded lonely, but he has these men friends he meets up with in London. There was no mention of neighbours ever entertained there, or of social outings the parents shared. I wondered if it's worthwhile contacting this Dr Toby Frobisher, since I have his work address.'

'It depends how far we're going to take this case. Officially, we do still have the three options open: accident, suicide or murder. Did you pick up what grounds the wife had for seeking a divorce?'

'No, I thought prying would stretch Joanna's loyalty too far. She's discreet by nature. It's only the emotional pressure that made her talk as freely as she did.'

Yeadings stayed silent, repeatedly reversing a pencil on his blotter, lead tip and eraser end alternately.

'We know exactly where she was when her husband fell,' Z reminded him gently.

'Yes. But, so far, we don't know whether she had found herself a lover and where he might have been at that moment. If Oliver suspected he was supplanted, he might have discussed it with his doctor friend. We'd be remiss if we didn't try to find out. Give him a ring, Z, and fix up a meeting.'

Chapter Twelve

Zyczynski's phone call was badly timed. Dr Toby Frobisher had an afternoon clinic, but, since the inquiry concerned the late Oliver Charrington, a sympathetic secretary promised he would get in touch immediately it was over. Z left her mobile number and decided to drive home. Beaumont had not returned from the first post-mortem and the CID office was empty, DC Silver having gone chasing up car registrations of locally licensed Audis.

At 8.34, Dr Frobisher phoned, apologising for the late hour. He was softly spoken with a deep unaccented voice. It wasn't too difficult to imagine lying relaxed on his couch for a session of psychic soothing.

He offered no information over the phone but explained that he had rescheduled his appointments for the next morning, had contacted Professor Littlejohn, and would be attending the post-mortem of his friend at Wexham Park Hospital.

'I hope to be there myself,' she told him, 'and I'd be grateful for a few minutes with you to discuss the case.

So far we're leaving our options open over how his death came about.'

'Certainly, Detective Sergeant. I shall be pleased to do anything to help.' Behind the assurance she seemed to hear a quiet addendum: 'within professional limits'. Dr Frobisher, by the very nature of his work, guaranteed discretion. And he was no dozer, having already been in touch with the pathologist for the time and place of the post-mortem, which was more than she knew yet herself.

She rang Beaumont but his mobile was switched off. She tried for him at home and Stuart took the call. 'He's in the shower, Z. Only just got in and he's heading for bed, dog-tired. Can I take a message?'

'It's just the time of tomorrow's PM on Oliver Charrington,' Z explained. 'I need to attend.'

'He'll be glad to let you take his place. Today's went on for ever. I think he said it's at 11 a.m. but I'll get him to confirm. OK?'

Good, she decided. There'd be time to put in her report before then, and attend any briefing Angus might arrange.

Unsurprisingly, Mott was mainly interested in Littlejohn's initial findings on the torched body. He had made a lightning visit to the car when it was *in situ* and made general observations. The woman's age was now narrowed to between twenty-eight and thirty-five. Her height would have been five foot seven inches. The only dental surgery had been on the capped lower left canine. There was no evidence of congenital defects or broken limbs, but the hyoid bone was fractured. The charred condition

158

of the flesh had not permitted any indication of whether strangulation had been manual or by ligature. Time of death was uncertain but had preceded the burning.

The reading of Professor Littlejohn's initial report was interrupted by the door bursting open as DC Silver came in, late and out of breath. 'Sorry,' he gasped. 'I think I've got a name for our body.'

'Sit and recover,' Mott offered. 'Is this in connection with the torched car?'

'The car's owner. Her name came up for a five-month old registration for that make and type, and now SOCO have confirmed the engine and chassis numbers. How do you fancy Margot Charrington?'

A stir went through the room. 'Our suicide's wife?' Beaumont demanded. 'You mean we could have the marital cliché? Husband kills wife and then does himself in? But that's all arse-about-face. He was already dead. We know Margot was in the studio when her husband fell from the grid on Friday. We all saw and spoke to her afterwards. If the burnt body is hers, she was put in the boot sometime between the Friday night and the early hours of Sunday when the car was torched. He certainly can't have done it.'

'So it's not a domestic, but it could still be her,' Yeadings cautioned. 'The age range is right. We need to check where her car is now. Z, have you found an address yet for where she's supposed to be staying?'

'No. I rang her home again and her mother's had no news. She's getting really anxious.'

'Dental records,' Mott snapped. 'DI Salmon, we need

those ASAP. And we'll need to know who saw her leave Telehouse after the party on Friday. I'll take Beaumont to check on where everyone headed off to. She may have mentioned the friends she was going to stay with. We'll need to question everyone again.'

'Try asking Athene,' Z suggested. 'She notices everything that goes on there. It could be one of the Telehouse people that Margot went home with. She would hardly have been in the mood to go to outsiders and start explaining what Oliver had just done.'

'If it is Mrs Charrington,' Yeadings warned them, 'her husband's death could be more than coincidence. We'll need to take a more thorough look at exactly how it happened. This means setting up an incident room at Telehouse. Who is attending his post-mortem?'

'I am.' Z held up a hand. 'It's at 11 o'clock. I've arranged to meet his doctor there for some background to the dead man's mental condition. Toby Frobisher was a close friend. They were at school together and kept in regular contact.'

Yeadings nodded. 'Good. I might even look in there myself. You can drive me.'

Professor Littlejohn was already in mask and apron, with a tall man in similar gear beside him, when they arrived. He introduced the man as Toby Frobisher with a string of impressive initials after his name. Superintendent Yeadings shook hands with him and presented Rosemary Zyczynski. All very formal and correct, she thought wryly. Now he's supposed to ask me for the next dance. Pardon my tarnished tiara.

'Shall we begin then?' Littlejohn suggested, almost jovial. He flicked a finger at the mike clipped to his apron to check it was live and signalled his assistant to uncover the body.

The surgical mask failed to hide the psychotherapist's pain. Doctor he might be, but this was alien country for him. Z could never doubt that the dead man had been his friend.

The body had been routinely cleaned to remove all congealed blood. The pathologist's assistant read off the dead man's name, age, weight and height. With an illuminated magnifier, Littlejohn spent long moments examining the exterior for bruising. He consulted his notes on the height of the guard rails of the grid and measured up from the body's naked feet. The waistline, palms of the hands, the wrists, front of elbows and upper arms were minutely gone over.

'There are no marks of ligatures or heavy manual bruising,' the pathologist declared. 'The face and upper cranium are badly damaged. There are multiple fractures of the cervical vertebrae consistent with a severe collision with a hard surface, but I find no evidence of strangulation.

It was not until the crushed chest cavity was opened and the organs separately removed for weighing that Frobisher overcame his distress enough to press forward for a closer look at the liver.

'A drinker.' Littlejohn murmured to him.

'Despite advice, and unwisely combined with prescription drugs. He knew it could only worsen his condition, but he chose to appear convivial among friends.

Alcohol's the great deceiver, I'm afraid. It fools the best of us.'

Littlejohn found nothing more remarkable about the inner organs. Last ingested food appeared to be a small amount of cereal; heart was on the large side, lungs quite good for his age, which had been given as fifty-two. 'No reason,' he said, 'why, with care, he shouldn't have carried on in the same way for another twenty years.'

Yeadings caught the flicker of pain in Frobisher's eyes. The man felt responsible for his friend's early death. He believed he had failed him.

'Things happen,' Yeadings said, 'that we can't possibly foresee.' But Frobisher moved away and appeared not to hear.

'Death,' the pathologist summed up, 'was, as ever, due to heart failure, accompanied here by multiple fractures and intensive internal bleeding. It was instantaneous and had not occurred before the body struck the floor.

'There remains, of course, the result of the toxicology tests, which should be available within four or five days. It is possible that they may offer some contributory reason for an accidental fall.'

Outside the mortuary, Yeadings decided not to wait for his DS in her car. 'Take your time with Frobisher,' he said. 'I'll get a taxi back. I think he'll find it easier to talk with you on your own.'

They found a table in the cafeteria and ordered tea, Zyczynski adding a request for scones, butter and strawberry jam. 'Good idea. I'll join you,' Frobisher said, smiling. 'It'll save wasting time on a late lunch.'

That hadn't been the DS's main intention. She had thought the physical preoccupation with buttering and jamming would do away with the need to meet the psychologist's eyes, which she found disconcerting. And she wasn't yet sure from what angle to start questioning him.

He made it easy for her. 'You know, I think, that Oliver was more than my patient. We had been a part of each other's lives since we were thirteen, an impressionable age.'

He stopped there, planting his buttered knife upright on its handle. 'Although, of course, every age is impressionable; certainly the stage Oliver had recently reached.

'His mother died in childbirth, so he never knew her. His father tried to fill the gap. He was certainly also the hero in Oliver's life, to an unusual degree because we all tend to see ourselves as the main hero of our own story. In a way, the father's over-importance diminished the son in his own eyes, so when Alex Charrington died Oliver's grief was almost beyond bearing.'

Psycho claptrap, Z thought. They always trace it back to the parents, don't they? From habit she asked, 'How did he die?'

'He drove to Beachy Head and kept straight on. The car was later retrieved from the sea and he was still strapped in it.'

She was shocked. 'So now, Oliver's death—'

'—could appear to be an echo of his father's.' Frobisher pushed his plate away, the buttered scone uneaten.

'It happened when Oliver's career was peaking. He

163

was certainly talented and had emerged from his habitual modest way of life into a blaze of stardom. On a surge of confidence he had proposed to Margot Gilbey, married her and they'd produced two children. His father had tried to hide his progressive instability but slowly, over the years, he had fallen into a state of manic depression, as it was then called. Exacerbated by alcohol abuse, it was incorrectly diagnosed as schizophrenia and after a violent outbreak in which he seriously wounded two complete strangers, he was sectioned, spending two years in an institution for the criminally insane. On release after re-diagnosis, he resumed drinking to excess, neglected to follow a recommended drug programme and finally decided to end his life. He left a letter to Oliver, which he destroyed immediately on first reading. No one else ever learnt of its contents.'

'And that caused Oliver's breakdown?'

'He was in a precarious state, but with instant support and understanding he could have recovered. We had lost touch while I was teaching at Monash University in Australia. I came back to find that Oliver, too, was confirmed as suffering from bi-polar disorder but was adamantly refusing to have Margot informed. He had transferred all his previous hero-worship for his father onto her, and kept up a charade in which she was his salvation, having taken over a parallel career to the one he was incapable of continuing.'

And, knowing his sad history, she had dismissed him simply as a depressive, Z remembered; as though he should just pull himself together and snap out of it.

'If he ever felt he was supplanted in the adored Margot's

affections, could that plunge him into a suicidal state?'

'You're asking if Margot had a lover?' He smiled. 'When could she ever find the time? Her career was everything to her. I've yet to come across such a single-minded woman. I doubt if ever the demands of domesticity or child-rearing gave her sleepless nights. She had everything faultlessly organised and delegated in her home life, as in her workaday one.

'Of course, given all that, there's nothing certain about the human psyche. At this mid-life period she could suddenly have discovered there were experiences beyond the familiar.'

Z's mobile sounded and she flipped a quick glance at the sender's identity. 'I'm sorry,' she said. 'My boss.'

'Please take it.'

She left the table and moved to a quiet corner. 'Sir?'

Briefly, Yeadings told her of a further development. The search for Margot Charrington's dental records had come up negative because her last check-up had been over six years ago. Meanwhile, her elderly dentist had died, leaving his records in total disorder and the members of the practice who followed him had not been able to find any reference to her. But, on the positive side, a twelve-year-old boy had been brought in by his father with the missing front licence plate from the wrecked car, picked up as a trophy during the early hours when the torching occurred. The lad had seen the blaze from his bedroom window and slipped out to investigate. The numbers further identified the Audi as belonging to Margot Charrington.

Z thanked him and returned to the table.

Frobisher picked up where he'd left off. 'I tried to help,' he admitted, 'but I failed. In addition to counselling I prescribed a succession of the usual drugs such as Prozac, lithium, amitryptyline, and so on. For a while they were beneficial. I had some success with Propanalol to control the manic phases, but Oliver had become too dependent on alcohol for boosting his belief in himself as a successful family man and a popular friend. His predisposition and the memory of his father's gradual decline were too strong in the end. I would like to believe his fall was partly accidental, but behind it there was surely lurking the belief that he must end as his father did.'

Their tea had cooled and they walked away leaving it almost untasted. They would be meeting again at the coroner's inquest, and until then Z felt uncertain which of the two men, living or dead, she felt most sympathy for.

She watched Dr Frobisher get into his car and drive from the parking area by the mortuary exit. How would he have felt, she wondered, if she'd told him that Margot Charrington had been left strangled and unrecognisable in her torched car? He'd held back from criticising her failure to care more for his friend, but privately how could he fail to blame her blindness to the suffering Oliver was unable to mask?

Angered, might he even have recognised a hint of justice in the callous way she had been disposed of so soon after her husband's suicide?

About to ease off the brake and follow him out, she gave herself a mental shake. Where had that unwelcome idea sprung from? She had to admit that the Job encouraged such cynicism, the suspicion that strangers she met on a case were all potential bad'uns. Perhaps, accustomed to dealing with skilled con-artists, she had underlying misgivings about his professional air of discretion.

So, on consideration, was Toby Frobisher, while grieving for his close friend, just a little too smooth? Too good to be true?

Chapter Thirteen

The next day's early morning meeting included the nuclear Serious Crimes CID and a selection of uniforms seconded for plain-clothes duty.

'We weren't to know Margot Charrington would get herself killed straight after we'd dealt with her husband; and his post-mortem still hasn't indicated whether his death was suicide or not,' Beaumont opened sourly. 'All we've got is this doctor friend's report on his precarious mental state. There's nothing to show he finally went over the edge.'

There was a titter from a uniform man at the unintentional pun. Over the edge was where Charrington had literally gone.

The early briefing had made Beaumont miss breakfast, and last night he'd been unable to contact any of the dead woman's colleagues. He scowled in the direction of the titter.

'The galling thing,' Mott summarised grimly, 'is that although we took addresses and phone numbers from everyone at the studios on Friday night, we let them disperse without querying where they could actually be found in the next few days. It's the end of a run for many of them and they've gone off for a deserved break, some with their mobiles switched off. It's only post-production who are still carrying on and they're up in Soho.

'At Telehouse, a whole new crowd were due to move in to record a pop video. It's all wild music, nubile girls and crotch-dancing, with a playback of fantastic effects including explosions and volcanoes. There's a minor riot because, with a double Charrington death, we've secured the studios as a crime scene for an intensive search, and it's doubling as the incident room.

'This new lot would bring in their own single film camera, vision and sound playback, so the only techs left over from the last few weeks would be the in-house lighting guys. With their senior man still in hospital, his assistant would be in charge. Except, of course, that we've closed the show down.'

Yeadings darted a look at his notes. 'Carl Winslow,' he recalled, 'quoted twice here as non-communicative. So possibly of little use for our purpose. Has anyone tried contacting Winslow?'

Beaumont grunted. 'Like most of the others, he's not answering his landline, sir. You're right that he'd not be very forthcoming. He's little short of a mute, couldn't get two words out consecutively when I questioned him on Friday.'

'It doesn't help that Margot arranged at short notice for her mother to step in while she went off with these unnamed friends,' Mott grumbled.

'Perhaps not such good friends, seeing how she ended up,' Beaumont doubted.

'I'm still in contact with Athene, the production assistant,' Z claimed. 'We're meeting up later. I'm hoping she may know where some of the others have gone. She did mention that Jamie, the floor manager, had planned a week's fell-walking in the north and hoped to take Jenny Barnes along with him, staying overnight wherever they ended up each day. Athene had sounded doubtful, though, about Jenny falling in with his invitation.'

'I guess so: walking would be out, now that she's sold on biking,' Silver put in.

'Yes, and I observed some hostility there,' Mott agreed. 'Jenny resents his masterful attitude. But I agree that Athene's probably the best source to tap for info. She's an observant woman and might dish any dirt on personal relations at Telehouse. She has implied that Margot wasn't everyone's favourite person.'

'That probably goes with the job description,' Z reminded them. 'Directors control the whole artistic set-up, and actors with oversize egos can resent criticism. I guess the techs are equally sensitive, professionals who don't take kindly to much bossing from the arty lot. A strong-willed woman, Margot was in the ideal position to override and make enemies. Also, with Jenny and Athene, she had a couple of lively younger women ready to walk into her shoes.'

Yeadings had stayed silent, but now he grunted. 'Not many of us commit murder to get promotion. And must we assume that she died at the hands of someone she worked with? Is there no chance that it was a random killing, an opportunist one-off? Suppose that on Friday night she stopped the car at a fake breakdown, to give a stranded driver a lift. That kind of ambush isn't uncommon.'

'Simply being in the wrong place at the wrong time? Victim of an attempted carjack? But, if so, why torch a valuable Audi, and where was it between then and the night of Saturday–Sunday?'

'Killing her might not have been intentional, just happening when she tried to fight back. Too much pressure on the neck, and suddenly you've a body to get rid of.'

'I'm not convinced she'd stop after dark to help a stranger. Maybe someone she knew guessed where she'd be heading and lay in wait. Do we know if she had friends out that way?'

Suggestions and questions were coming in thick and fast, but none of them leading anywhere; only widening supposition to allow that anyone in the wide world might have taken Margot Charrington's life.

'Every CCTV and speed camera footage within a twenty-mile radius is being examined for the night of Friday–Saturday,' Mott said, bringing them down to practicalities. It's a long shot, but the Audi may have been carjacked in some urban street, although the next night's dumping ground was isolated. There's a blank for the vital end of the journey.

'We have to narrow down the whole situation to basic possibilities. Are we dealing with three individual incidents within thirty-six hours: Oliver's suicide or accident, Margot's murder, and the car-torching? Were they committed by separate parties? Or could the three be linked, even through cause and effect?'

There was a moment's silence while the second option was considered. 'Surely it's too far-fetched to assume Oliver Charrington's death sparked off his wife's murder,' Beaumont doubted.

Zyczynski recalled her way-out notion about Frobisher: how he'd implied Margot was to blame in failing to recognise his old friend's precarious mental state and offer support. That the doctor could react viciously had been only a split-second suspicion and she refused to share it with the others now.

But a strange anomaly stuck in her mind. Frobisher had insisted that Oliver was devoted to his wife and placed her on a pedestal. Yet, if he had intended to take his own life, how could he have borne to inflict the sight of it on her? They needed now to look further into that evening at the studios, to see if any third party had a reason to want both Charringtons dead.

'There's an enormous canvas to cover,' Yeadings admitted. 'We can augment the team with up to fifty uniforms for immediate inquiries, but I'll need to call in CID back-up from other Areas. And we've nothing useful yet from forensics. Dabs on the licence plate proved only that the local lad who picked it up was a stranger to soap and water. Any partials underneath are smudged; and there's nothing left on the car to lead us to whoever last drove it.

'Z, it looks as though we're relying on your meeting with Athene to dig up something useful on Margot Charrington's private life.'

'Or from her mother. I'm going out there to question her as soon as we've finished here,' Mott offered.

The meeting broke up. Beaumont, leaving the building, recognised Patsy Carter of the *Courier* in the driving seat of a blue Renault parked in a slot reserved for chief inspectors. He walked across and she lowered her window. 'I've only temporarily promoted myself,' she explained, grinning.

Beaumont declined to see the joke. 'Don't hang around,' he told her. 'There's nothing for you, except to give the police a bad name. PR office will be issuing press handouts in our good time.'

'Oh, come on. Give a girl a hint. Two juicy deaths in thirty-six hours. Our public deserves a little reassurance that the police aren't sleeping on the job. We know who the suicide is. Are you still in the dark about the incinerated woman?'

'You'll have to wait for a press statement, Patsy.'

'Ah, so I can say the police have a name for her and they're sitting on it?'

'I didn't say that.'

'You as good as did. Thanks, honeybun.'

Beaumont glared and walked on. She watched him unlock his red Toyota and sit waiting for her to drive off. In no hurry, she noted. That meant that right now he wasn't following a vital lead.

But Z and DCI Mott were. Both came out shrugging their coats on as they made for their own cars. She had a choice of which to follow and picked on the senior officer, certain she'd been right when a woman PC ran out to join

174

him. This looked like official preparation to break bad news. If she trailed them discreetly she'd arrive at some address connected with the torched woman. With luck she'd manage an interview with the family after they left, and get a name to print in this evening's edition.

Athene Devereux lived in a modern, two-storey brick and glass house on the edge of a recently built estate. It was little more than dolls' house-size and immaculately kept. A tiny front garden was laid down to grass. There were imported yellow roses in a crystal vase on the sitting-room table and a smell of freshly roasted coffee beans wafting in from the galley-sized kitchen. Z assumed that she lived alone and liked it that way.

'I've been racking my memory for anything unusual happening in that week of the final recordings,' Athene said, opening the subject directly as she carried in a tray for elevenses.

'Until that thing with Oliver, I mean. It's always pretty hectic as we near the end in a series, but it did seem that everyone was a bit more wired than usual.'

'Including Margot?'

'More than anyone, I'd say. It's none of my business, and perhaps I shouldn't discuss it, but now that this is a murder case, for you police every detail must be significant.'

'Was she uptight? Apprehensive?'

'No, rather the opposite. She's never lacked confidence, but those last two or three days it was as though…she was incandescent: nothing was impossible. This was after she'd got Roger to work on his inserts. And Greg's script revision was absolutely right: it was a great way of finishing him off, on a cliff-hanger.'

'I'm afraid you've lost me. I understand how a cliff-hanger works, but this Roger and his inserts?'

'I'm sorry. Of course, you haven't seen either the original or the amended script. Roger has played the station officer throughout the series, and Greg, the producer, felt he was as interesting as cold unsalted porridge. In fact, he wanted him gone. So he consulted with the scriptwriters and, for a touch of pathos, he inserted the hint of a love affair in the offing. Then, at the next call-out, Roger was to be crushed under a falling beam. The finale had him trolleyed off unconscious, covered in blood and wearing a neck brace. In the first episode of the new series he'll be featured as a floral-decked casket surmounted with his white helmet. A formal funeral, and thereafter a more eye-catching actor as station officer.

'Like most of us, Roger hadn't seen this coming, and he went berserk when he was notified. Well, understandably. Of course, it was Greg who insisted on the script changes, and on principle Margot opposed them at such a late stage, until she saw she could make it all work. By then Greg had tactically withdrawn.'

'Leaving Margot to take the flak?'

'Guiding Roger through rehearsal and run-throughs before final recording. It was a lot to get done in the given time and she pulled it off brilliantly.'

But with a fresh enemy added to the list, Z noted silently. 'Margot wasn't worried about repercussions?'

'I'm sure that didn't occur to her. I told you, she was

176

super-confident by this stage: aglow with her own success.'

Athene busied herself with pouring the coffee. 'Sorry I've no biscuits,' she apologised.

'Really, this is fine. Was anyone else behaving in an unusual way?'

'There was one thing.' Athene paused, cafetiere balanced in one hand. 'I noticed Jenny—'

Z waited. 'What about Jenny?'

'During the break, when Margot almost gave up on Roger, Jenny took Roger off somewhere private and sorted him out. Heaven knows what persuasion she used, but he returned a different man. It wasn't just due to Margot's skilled direction. He came up with a feeling for the part that none of us was expecting.'

'Perhaps the desperation of a final throw?'

'A *tour de force*. Not the dull old Roger we'd known. And for that matter, not the Jenny we knew, either. She's really another Margot in the making, cool-headed, detached. I'd never seen the sympathetic side of her before. Whatever she said to boost his confidence, she wrought magic on Roger.'

'You were watching her closely at the time.'

'Yes, because of something she did just before she marched Roger off. She had no obvious reason for it, you see. I wondered why she needed to slide away behind the cyc. Maybe a broken shoulder-strap; some adjustment she needed a bit of privacy for. She was only gone for a couple of minutes. The stand-in lighting gaffer must have noticed too, because he went in after her, as if checking what she was up to.'

177

'This lighting tech? He'd be…?'

'Carl Winslow. He'd taken over because his boss was off on sick leave. I don't really know him. Well, I don't suppose anyone does. He's quite a cold fish, doesn't mix at all.'

'No chance that it was a secret assignation?'

Athene chuckled. 'They'd have nothing in common. Jenny wouldn't notice a grey ghost like him. No, probably he was just checking that she didn't trip over his cables.'

'In case Jenny went up as far as the grid?'

'She's not allowed up there. And, anyway, why would she want to?'

It seemed of no importance, but Z made a note all the same. 'Were they talking together when they came back?'

'No, Jenny was first to return, and Carl a couple of minutes later from a different opening. Maybe they never saw each other behind there. There are several breaks in the cyc, which goes all the way round the walls, and there's more than one stairway.'

'I'll need to speak to them both, because of Oliver Charrington's fall later. They may have noticed if anyone else was up there.'

Athene frowned. 'This was a long time earlier. No one admits to observing when Oliver arrived. And everyone was stuck at their post during the whole of the final shoot. I'm sure Oliver would have been up there alone.'

'And when recording was finished, how much time elapsed between people moving off and Oliver hitting the ground?'

Athene looked appalled. 'It's impossible to say precisely.

But you're not thinking one of us went up there and pushed him off? That just wouldn't happen. Everyone liked Oliver.'

'Was there time?'

'It was chaos, with everyone clearing their stuff before rushing along to the party. At a wild guess, I'd say there was anything between seven and twelve minutes before the floor was almost clear of people working below.'

'And was anyone noticed going behind the cyc during that time?'

'Most unlikely, given the pressures. It was after Oliver fell that people came rushing back to look.'

'So where was Margot the last time you saw her before it happened?'

'Still up in the gallery, talking to Nicco. They'd... they'd eyes only for each other.' Athene looked down at her hands, unwilling to go on.

Z waited, until the silence between them became almost unbearable.

At last Athene sighed and gave in. 'It had been getting more obvious over those last two days,' she admitted. 'Something was happening between them.'

Margot was aglow, she'd said before. So was this something Oliver too could have been observing from his high perch on the grid? Did he suspect his perfect wife of taking this younger man as her lover?

Mott had found Mrs Gilbey already wild-eyed and desperate. When he broke the news to her that her daughter's Audi had been identified as the burnt-out car described in the local paper, she became hysterical, torn between disbelief that Margot could have been killed and panic over how she could pick up the pieces. She seemed to have forgotten that Oliver ever existed, let alone was gone too.

After he had poured her a brandy she struggled to control herself. 'They'll have to go to boarding school,' she protested, 'and I must put this huge house up for sale to cover expenses. But it's not a seller's market now. Then there'll be the holidays. I can't be expected to take them in at my place now that I've downsized.'

Mott assumed she referred to the grandchildren. 'How are they taking their father's death?' he asked.

'How do you expect? They're distraught. Miranda keeps throwing things about and shouting. Charlie's the opposite; he won't say anything. Won't even eat. Well, none of us has much appetite anyway. God only knows how I'll break it to them about their mother.'

She lapsed into silence, tearing at a lace-edged handkerchief between nervous fingers. When she spoke again it was barely above a murmur. 'I'll have to keep the child-minder on, for a while at least. God knows what savings Margot has put by to support them.'

She turned on Mott. 'I suppose Dr Frobisher may know who Oliver's executors are; but I can't imagine Margot ever making a will. She'd certainly not expected to die so soon.'

She sat huddled and tearful. At last the inevitable thought came. She shook her head, eyes closed and lips trembling. 'You never think, do you, it could happen like this? It's…indecent, losing a child when you're…well, still here yourself.'

Mott remained there long enough to believe the woman was getting a grip on herself. She had refused to allow the policewoman to stay on for support. There was the child-minder – or would be, when she returned from taking Miranda and Charlie to the park. Neither had felt up to facing school.

They saw themselves out, leaving Carlotta propped against cushions on a sofa by the window. It was starting to rain gently with scattered snowflakes that turned instantly to water on the car's bonnet. Mott switched on the wipers and lights before pulling away from the kerb, unaware of the watcher in a blue Renault parked fifty yards to the rear.

Patsy Carter was disappointed at where they'd led her. This was obviously some unfinished business over Oliver Charrington's suicide. But if they'd needed to take it a step further, maybe she too could get more information by tackling Mrs Gilbey now. A real bonus would be if Margot had returned home and was willing to grant an exclusive interview about her ex-celebrity husband.

She waited a further ten minutes before pulling into the horseshoe drive and ringing the front doorbell.

Mike Yeadings wandered along to the PR office and unearthed the civilian in charge there from her scanning of a mound of tabloid newspapers.

'Got something for us, Superintendent?' she asked eagerly.

'Not for immediate distribution, but I want you to set up a press meeting here for tomorrow at 9 a.m. That will allow time to catch the mid-morning TV and local radio news. Also the early afternoon nationals.'

'Have you got someone for the car torching?'

'Possibly a name for the body,' he said cautiously.

'Will you take the meeting yourself, sir?'

'I'll be working with DCI Mott on the wording of the statement. He will be the official spokesman, backed on either side by Sergeants Beaumont and Zyczynski.'

'And Detective Inspector Salmon, sir?' she asked with mock innocence.

Yeadings had been expecting the question. Not only was Salmon's fishily down-turned mouth un-photogenic, but he was famously short on respect for journalists of any brand. To his mind, there was only one direction in which questions could be directed, and that with him as inquisitor.

'I'll look in on proceedings at some point,' Yeadings assured her. 'And find a seat at the back.'

He returned to his office and started to draft a statement making the most of the sparse progress on both cases. At least he'd have one chunk of raw meat to fling to the lions. Once they'd seized on both victims being the Charringtons they'd be raring to rush back and delve into the ready-prepared obituaries kept regularly updated on local celebrities, then rush out the banner headlines.

He had the statement shaped up for Mott to see and went off for an early lunch in the Mess, where a visiting member from the Royal Canadian Mounted Police was being entertained by his chief super. It was mildly disappointing that he wasn't in romantic operetta uniform and carolling for Rose Marie.

Yeadings was considering the relative merits of the cheeseboard and raspberry pavlova when his mobile vibrated. He read off the duty sergeant's message. 'I think you should take this, sir.'

'Excuse me,' he said and left the table.

It was as well. The phone call put through to him was explosive.

'Hello, is that Superintendent Yeadings?' an infuriated female voice spat in his ear. 'This is Margot Charrington. I want to report my car stolen.'

Chapter Fourteen

There was a brief silence, but not by a flicker did Yeadings's expression change. 'Mrs Charrington, I'd been hoping you would get in touch. We have news of your car and there are two or three points we need cleared up. I'd like you to come in. One of my sergeants will pick you up, if you'll tell us where you are.'

He reached for a notebook and Mott pushed a pen into his hand. 'The Falcon Inn, Denham Village,' he repeated. 'Yes, I know it: over the hump-backed bridge and almost immediately on the right. Half an hour, shall we say?'

He replaced the receiver and regarded his team wryly. 'And last night she was a charred corpse, according to our highly reliable *Courier*. I ask myself where they sourced their information. Can anyone here enlighten me?'

Beaumont stuck out his chin aggressively. 'That bloody Patsy Carter was hanging around. I gave her short shrift, but she must have picked up something after we left.'

'We could have done without this embarrassment. The top brass won't take it too kindly, especially if the press turn on us for implying false information. It will mean my wasting time over at Kidlington, sorting it with the AC; but let's get this interview set up first. Since it's me she contacted, I'll need to be present. Angus, do you want to sit in, or shall we leave it to whoever fetches her?'

'Zyczynski,' Mott said shortly. 'Get across there sharpish. I'll simply draft a couple of questions, sir.'

'Right, guv.' Z retrieved her notebook and slipped the elastic band over it. If she was quick Mott would have time to shape up a positive statement for the press release.

'I think, Angus,' Yeadings mused aloud, 'we'll make it informal, in my office, and you can happen to drop in. It will help the lady relax; she's probably embarrassed about explaining her disappearance.'

'Bereavement does funny things to us,' Beaumont murmured sarcastically, staring at the ceiling. 'I'll put a fiver on it: the widow was off celebrating with lover boy.'

Yeadings collected his papers together and removed his reading glasses. 'I didn't hear that,' he said, quitting the room.

What Z noticed first as she collected Margot from the cosy bar of the Falcon was that her make-up was heavier than before and her eyes puffy with lack of sleep. She still wore the same outfit as at Telehouse on Friday night, but now there was a dark stain on the front of her sweater, and her tailored jeans had acquired a teenager's sloppiness. Just to sort herself out and get a change of clothes she must be more than ready to go home.

Except, of course, that her mother would be waiting for her with a barrage of questions and recrimination.

She was in no mood for conversation with the DS, not even asking after the state of her car. She downed the remains of her scotch, grabbed her coat and walked out of the pub, leaving Z to follow. Where are we going, Sergeant?' She let herself into the front passenger seat, not willing to look like a suspect.

'Mr Yeadings's team is working out of Maidenhead at present.'

'Right.' And that was all until they reported to the duty sergeant and waited for Yeadings to send down for them. Meanwhile, they sat on the visitors' bench in reception, Margot's eyes closed as she worked out how little she could manage to admit to.

'Mrs Charrington, how are you?' Yeadings asked solicitously as she was ushered in.

'Bloody but unbowed.' The attempt at humour fell flat. Yeadings let Z fill two mugs from his cafetiere which had been burbling on the windowsill behind him. Margot took the chair indicated and blinked in the winter sunlight.

'Yeadings read out her car licence number from a card on his desk. 'Where would it have been taken from?' he asked.

'Telehouse car park, where I'd left it on Friday morning.' Her tone was sharp, as if cutting off any further details. 'Where was it found?'

He explained, adding that it was badly damaged by fire: certainly an insurance write-off. This appeared to be news to her but she was barely surprised.

'That's what they usually do, isn't it? Speed around until they crash it, then fire it and run away. And *if* they get

187

caught, all they'll get is a slap on the wrist. The law on prosecuting minors needs revision.'

'Who do you mean by "they"?'

'Well, kids, of course. Joyriding, though we shouldn't glamorise them by calling it that. It's aggravated theft, pure and simple.'

'But Telehouse car park has a security lodge and the electronic gates are kept closed. Enterprising youngsters might climb over to get in, but how could they drive out something as large as your Audi? I understand that only security have access by card. Everyone else employed there is issued with a visitor's pass and its colour is changed weekly. Perhaps your Audi went out in a stream of other vehicles, without the gate guard observing who was driving. But in that case, surely someone at that time would have noticed a stranger breaking in and hot-wiring the car? Unless you gave someone a second set of keys? I assume you still hold your own?'

'Of course I do, and the spare set is at my home in Great Missenden. But does it matter how? The damage is done. I'll have to replace the car. It's most inconvenient at the moment.'

A knock on the door introduced Angus with a sheaf of papers in one hand. He apologised for the interruption, but Yeadings waved him to a spare chair. 'I think you've met our DCI Mott. Angus, Mrs Charrington was asking why it matters how her car came to go missing. Perhaps you'd explain.'

'The main reason,' Mott said calmly, 'is that we found a body in the boot.'

Her arm twitched and hot coffee spilt over, soaking her trousers. Z sprang forward with a box of tissues.

'I don't understand,' Margot said, wincing at the scald and fiercely dabbing away at her thigh. 'How could that be?'

'It was a woman's body,' Yeadings said. 'And because you owned the car the press have assumed it was yours.'

Shakily Margot placed the part-emptied mug on the edge of the superintendent's desk, where Z eased a cork mat under it.

'So whose was it?'

Yeadings let a silence build.

'You must know, surely, by now?'

'With your phone call, Mrs Charrington, we were relieved to learn you're alive. Sadly, the body was beyond recognition.'

Margot drew a deep breath. 'Well, it has nothing to do with me. Wait a minute; you said it was *in the boot*? Do you mean she wasn't killed in the crash? But that doesn't make sense.'

'Can you help us to make sense of it?'

She was appalled. 'Somebody had to put her in there, maybe killed her. Oh my God; do you think they mistook her for me?'

'Well,' Yeadings demanded after both women had left, 'do we believe it was total news to her?'

'Given her job,' Mott said grimly, 'with so much rehearsing of others, acting would come easily enough. And she's had time to think up a suitable story. Interesting how quick she was to ask what the cameras had picked up in Telehouse car park. When you said the car was filmed leaving, but that the driver was obscure, I'd almost have accepted her annoyance as genuine. But was there a shade of apprehension before she asked?'

A light tap sounded at the door and Z was back. 'Do you need me, sir?'

'Certainly, we would value your opinion. What did you make of the lady's reactions?'

'Right now she's not enchanted with being sent home in a patrol car. And in here there was something I did notice. Although her make-up was really thick, I'm pretty sure that the sunlight showed up dark bruises underneath, over the left cheekbone and temple. They could be over twenty-four hours old. I believe she was punched hard at least twice. Who would have done that to her; or was she actually injured in the car accident?

'Also I'd question whether she'd been staying over in Denham Village since leaving Telehouse on Friday night. If so, why hadn't she gone out to shop for some overnight things? Uxbridge stores are near enough. She hadn't so much as a large handbag with her, let alone a change of clothes.'

Mott nodded. 'Her stories don't add up. I accept she hadn't intended to stay away from home Friday night, but then her husband fell from the grid. To us she claimed she'd needed space, to be alone; presumably to face what had happened. But she rang her mother to say she was staying with friends. Where were they when you picked her up? And if she left her car behind, who was it that gave her a lift?'

'And in your report of yesterday, Z, we find the observant Athene Devereux suspected she was starting, or about to start, an affair with one of the young technicians,' Yeadings recalled.

'Niccolo Facci – he has an Italian father – a cameraman working on the series with her. He'll be her camera one when they start shooting the sequel, because his boss retired on Friday. Margot's recommendation had sealed Niccolo's promotion.'

'So let's suppose they were holed up together over the weekend, and they had something more than a lovers' tiff,' Mott suggested. 'Or must we also consider others who felt Margot had messed things up for them? This retiring camera boss, for example; or the actor Roger who had suddenly been written out? Could either have lain in wait and attacked her?'

'Given the nature of the job,' Yeadings agreed, 'Margot could have more enemies at Telehouse than friends. Others there could feel as passionate about their careers as she does.'

'Enemies other than just there,' Z murmured. If they were listing those with grudges, however slight, she now felt she must mention her passing doubt about Toby Frobisher.

'Oliver's doctor was his lifetime friend. They were really close, from schooldays, and I believe he feels bitter over Oliver's final breakdown: blaming Margot, if not for actually driving him to desperation, but at least for refusing him the encouragement and support he badly needed. Without accusing her openly, he seemed to think she repaid his devotion with callous indifference. She struck me too as having little patience with anyone outside her own career interests.'

'You're not attributing your personal prejudices to him, are you, Z?' Mott suggested.

Zyczynski's face froze. 'I try to be objective.' Admittedly she was as affected by personal chemistry as anyone. She'd liked Toby Frobisher on first sight, and there was a lot about Margot Charrington that really raised her hackles.

'I'm just reminding you that she did have contacts outside her job. She could have been just as harsh to those people.'

The internal phone rang on the coffee-cluttered desk. 'Yeadings,' he said, lifting it. He listened for a few seconds. 'Right, let's see them.'

'That was Beaumont,' he told the others. 'He's just back from conducting an intensive search of the studios at Telehouse, and he's come up with some interesting objects.'

They waited in silence, Yeadings nodding to Mott to set the door ajar. They heard approaching footfalls and Beaumont came bustling in, a gleam of success in his eyes.

'There's good news and not so good news,' he told them, planting a brown carrier bag on the desk. 'Does it matter where I start?'

'The good news,' Yeadings demanded.

Beaumont produced a see-through evidence bag. It contained a mobile phone. 'Two techs working in the studios have identified this as belonging to Margot Charrington. It had fallen into a dark crevice in the grid, beside a coiled rope. This was close to the point where her husband had been standing before he fell. There are smudges all over it, at least two separate sets of dabs overprinted by the late Oliver's.

'The battery was flat, so I've had it recharged. The screen was shattered but we've been able to bring up what we needed. Her last voicemail was from Nicco Facci. It's personal, even intimate. Would you care to hear it?'

Yeadings nodded and they listened in uncomfortable silence as the young man described in lurid detail just how he intended celebrating with her at the end of the shoot.

Beaumont clicked the phone shut. 'There's other stuff, referring to earlier exploits.' He looked round with satisfaction at the watching faces.

'You say Oliver Charrington was the last person to touch this?' Mott pursued.

'His prints show he'd opened some messages, yes. And the mobile was discovered where he might have thrown it down. As you can see, it's quite damaged.'

'Well, re-bag it for the coroner's office,' Yeadings told him sombrely. 'It should make his decision a whole lot simpler. And what's your other news?'

'We could have a subsidiary plot to mystify us. SOCO has turned up a stash of Class A drugs, mainly coke and heroin, some Ecstasy, hidden in one of those cable boxes halfway up the stairs to the grid. It's with forensics at present being assessed. It's not a wholesale supply, but certainly more than a personal stash. We could have a dealer working at Telehouse, probably a profitable market, given the reputation of some TV celebrities. There are no identifiable prints on the plastic wrapping, but they're testing for traces of fabric or latex gloves.'

Chapter Fifteen

The stalker stood in the pouring rain and waited for the girl to appear. Despite the overcast sky there were no lights on in the upstairs apartment. He knew she wasn't at the market because he'd trawled it several times for sight of the green bobble hat which she would certainly have worn in weather like this. There had been other headgear, mostly rainproof, showing streaky blond hair underneath, like the wig he'd recently watched her buy; but nowhere that sleek, short red hair peeking out over her pert little nose and china-blue, innocent eyes.

But were they so innocent? Over these weeks of watching, misgivings had started to creep in. The wig still worried him. Why did she need it? Was it a disguise, as though she knew he was out here waiting and she meant to tease him? He'd seen her wearing it only once, under the skid lid. Before she got on the bike she'd spread the blond hair over her shoulders, smiling secretly around, as if challenging anyone to notice and associate it with her. And then the bike; it was so out of character, suggesting someone quite different – almost diametrically the opposite of the girl he knew was for him. It was too daring, unwomanly.

He imagined her now, astride it, speeding up some motorway in this deluge, vulnerable to other traffic, on a grease-slicked surface; and his heart thudded with apprehension. She shouldn't take risks, not with other people. Didn't she realise the dangers out there? She was making herself risk-prone, when she had only to turn to him and accept he was there to take care of her, shelter her for ever. There were terrible contradictions in her which disturbed him while being at the same time alluring, because they made him need to dig deeper, find out more about this enigmatic woman waiting for him to claim her.

Through the plate glass windows of the picture-framing shop he could see two late customers, one slowly circling to admire the paintings for sale, the other going to great lengths over selecting a mount and frame for some amateur daub. The elderly man who ran the shop was more than adequately occupied.

It was something he'd already once accomplished after dark, but today, deprived of sight of her, he needed it so much more: to be there with her possessions ranged all around him. He needed to touch them, run silky fabrics through his fingers, inhaling from garments that had been intimate with her flesh; drink from glasses and cups that her lips had closed on; lie in the sheets she had lain in perhaps wonderfully naked.

He stood at the neighbouring street entrance, breathless with excitement, hands trembling so that he feared he might not manage to deal with the outer lock and then the flight of stairs to her door. But the rain helped, driving people off the street, and those who did scurry past had their heads down, making for home or the temporary refuge of the nearby Starbucks. There was no one to see as he produced his battery power drill and inserted it in the lock.

It was a different one this time, but nothing complicated. The drill drove through. Poor quality metal. Her landlord had been out to save a penny, risking untold dangers to the precious girl he was there to protect. Ignorant fool! It would serve him right if later he detected sounds from the floor above and came up to investigate. Then he should see what dangers his crass folly and meanness could cause.

Once inside, for whole minutes he sat on the top of the stairs until his breathing became normal. It wouldn't do to walk in while he was so... So *what*? Out of control? But he wasn't that. He was totally *in* control. Masterful. If he found she was actually there, maybe resting in bed, she should see how completely he would take over, care for her, prepare her a hot drink, a wonderful meal, and much, much more. She would see how inevitable it was, his claim, after he'd denied himself for so long and with such superhuman patience.

He dealt in the same way with this lock. All his passion went into the single thrust against the metal. Again, the cheap mechanism gave way. This was a vastly superior means of entry to the crude way he'd broken in before.

He needed their sanctuary kept secure. In a day or two he'd go out and buy a new, more powerful lock; order just two keys; make sure the feckless fellow downstairs was denied access in future.

He pushed the door ajar and listened. There was no cry of surprise or protest. Was she waiting silently, ready to reach for him?

The apartment was empty. He walked all the way through: the diminutive, white-painted hall with its four closed doors opening on to a sitting room, bathroom, kitchen, and finally bedroom. There came a flash of disappointment – even suspicion that she was mocking him. But later, picking up glass fragments from the pots of make-up he'd furiously swept from her dressing-table top, he realised how opportune this delay was. There was so much he could prepare before his darling came home to him. He would make the whole place sing with welcome.

Mott's curiosity had been sufficiently aroused to send him straight to Telehouse to see where the drugs had been hidden. He had left examination of the lower levels behind the cyc to SOCO, and only now saw the extent of the problem. The surface of the walls all around the studio were concealed by black curtaining which reached as far up as tilted camera shots were likely to reach. Above the curtains stretched high, concrete breeze-block walls punctuated by large junction boxes of battleship grey.

There were a hundred places where the drugs might have been stashed without danger of disturbance. Mott was shown one of several metal boxes covered with greasy dust where smudges marked a spring-loaded catch with a loop permitting use of a small padlock, now removed. Its condition suggested it could have remained unopened for a matter of years.

A white-overalled woman from SOCO came up behind him. 'This is where we found the stuff,' she told him.

Mott shone his torch in. The box was empty now. He climbed up into the grid itself, making his way cautiously. On the walkway, past a mechanism for the lighting hoists, a yellow police marker with a black number 3 indicated where Margot's mobile phone had been found. Close by was another marked 2, which showed where Oliver had stood before going over the rail. Rings were chalked round the points where powder deposits had brought up his fingerprints as he gripped it with both hands. No.1 marker, Mott recalled, was below, where the body had struck the studio floor.

Nothing up here left much to the imagination. Since the mobile phone had given up its last messages the story was complete. The whole area seemed saturated with despair. Mott was glad to go down again to the more wholesome challenge of puzzling why, when the teams working on the *All Fired Up* series were about to disband, valuable drugs should have been left for a police search to uncover.

It would have been in the timing. Athene had described how Oliver's dramatic fall brought everyone running back to the studio floor. This crowd of possible witnesses would have warned off the dealer from making a dash to recover the stuff. He, or she, had left it too late, because the floor manager, Greg, had all approaches to the grid's stairways roped off at once.

But since then there had surely been opportunities for

anyone who'd had a reason to return. Although it was a secured crime scene, a limited number of Telehouse security guards and certain of the techs had been allowed in to take care of equipment. They could be eliminated as the dealer, since the stash had remained unclaimed. The suspect must be among those who were missing, someone running a profitable second career at the studios.

It offered a sizeable cast. A speedier approach might be to trace the dealer through his customers. Users of Class A drugs were notoriously incautious about covering up their habit. Among people like these, they might even have enjoyed flaunting their bohemian lifestyle. Someone should have noticed.

Already Mott was cautious about relying on Athene Devereux for so much past information. Such a super-efficient person could have been behind the drugs business and, anyway, opinions and evidence from a single source must have a personal slant. Unfortunately, so many of those who might have observed or suspected a drug habit existing alongside the legitimate business of Telehouse were temporarily out of reach. Who remained that he could question about this?

Superintendent Yeadings was under pressure from his AC Operations to clear the crime scene at Maidenhead and let work resume there. The coroner who was to hold the inquest on Oliver Charrington had seen no need to summon a jury on what now appeared a straightforward choice between accident and suicide. So an official visit by bus to examine the site was not required. He would demand only identification of the dead person and an explanation of the circumstances surrounding the finding of the body, before adjourning the court for a fortnight. There remained no reason for holding up operations vigorously being pushed by the governing board at Telehouse.

However, now that the discovery of the drugs stash had opened a separate crime inquiry there, Yeadings drove across to Kidlington in torrential rain to argue his position in person.

Over Lapsang Souchong served with fine lemon slices, he wickedly let slip that the scheduled next production at Telehouse, at present delayed, would be a pop video by the riotous Terminal Fuction group, who were presently celebrating the withdrawal of charges against three of its members for affray and GBH, due to the disappearance of two vital witnesses.

'Not that it affects the situation in any way,' Yeadings murmured urbanely.

'Er, quite.' The AC stirred his tea, considered the spoon solemnly and decided to add a small white tablet as sweetener. He was a classical music lover and now felt confirmed in his decision to return the ten complimentary tickets to view future recordings at the studios.

'This quantity of drugs,' he mused. 'It seems unlikely to have been abandoned completely. Are you convinced that the person responsible for it was involved in the production you mentioned – er, *All Fired Up*, was it?'

'I doubt it was left over from any previous programme, given a street value of over nine hundred pounds. While we're pulling in hauls of thousands, even millions these days, it may seem small beer, but identifying a source is vitally important.'

'Oh, I agree, Superintendent, but could this not be an advance delivery for this next, pop video lot – Terminal Function?'

'*Fuction*,' Yeadings corrected blandly. 'They probably have their own supplies elsewhere and better protected. No, in view of where the stock was hidden, I believe we have to look among the technicians who had access to the rear of the cyc and the grid. There are hoists for the lighting and other electrical equipment there serviced by Telehouse's own technicians. If we allowed the pop video to proceed, they would have access again and would be able to cover their tracks. I need the studios closed down until we have searched further.'

'Oh, I see. Yes, quite.'

The AC offered a refill from his Worcestershire teapot, which Yeadings politely declined. 'Well, Telehouse must accept, Superintendent, that police requirements do have priority. You have made your point.'

Examination of the wrecked Audi Cabriolet, ownership of which had already been confirmed through undamaged engine and chassis numbers, now revealed the origin and cause of its incineration. With no evidence to suggest skidding on the road or heavy collision with other traffic, it appeared to have been driven at full speed into the tree, which demolished its headlights and front valance; detached the licence plate; crumpled the bonnet and sprang its lid, shattering the windscreen. The two front airbags had been deployed on impact but were destroyed in the subsequent fire.

Small chunks of charred brick removed from the floor near the driving seat had been analysed and weighed, approximating to the mass of a standard builder's-brick. Experiments in the forensic science labs were being carried out to demonstrate how one might have been loaded on the pedal and fixed to obtain maximum acceleration.

'You needn't search for an injured driver,' the boffin assured Silver by phone. 'At the time of the crash there wasn't one. Just as well, because look what it did to a good, honest, kiln-fired brick!'

Silver reported to DI Salmon, who made the nearest-ever approach to a joke known to have left his down-turned mouth. 'And everyone carries a brick with them, in case need arises.'

'And the fire,' Silver continued to retail, 'was as supposed: liberal quantities of ordinary lead-free petroleum as supplied at every pump in the country: then, of course, application of struck matches, flaming rag or other equivalent. Three distinct points of origin were found, one of them definitely the fuel-soaked contents of the boot.'

While Salmon continued to sit silent, apparently seeking inspiration from the scarred wood grain on the top of his desk, Silver was left soberly wondering what any poor cow could have done to deserve such a through and vicious despatch.

From some accounts it should have been Margot Charrington, owner of the Audi and widow of the suicide. She was known to have upset a number of people. So had the killer been an agent sent to kill her and he'd mistaken one woman for another? It would have been the simpler solution, except that then they'd have two to hunt down and charge with the murder.

Whether his thoughts had been running on a parallel track or simply converged, DI Salmon muttered as if to himself, 'Snapped hyoid bone.' He faced Silver severely. 'It could have been accidental,' he said as if in accusation. 'Then somebody panicked, left with a body to dispose of.'

So whose? Silver asked himself. Best thing he could do was take another good look at the CCTV pictures from Telehouse car park. Maybe by now the nerds had done something useful with enhancing. So much depended on the identity of the person driving Margot's abandoned car.

Rosemary Zyczynski had followed Margot home a bare half hour later. By the time she arrived she hoped that the two women's tempers would have flared and died out somewhat. Joanna answered the door. From somewhere in the recesses behind her a child was shouting at the top of its voice.

'Not now,' the woman warned. 'Whatever you want, just drop it. No comment, whoever you are. There's nobody here.'

She spun on her axis and hissed viciously, 'Miranda, for heaven's sake shut up. Or you'll wake Grandma.'

Grandma who wasn't here? If the child-minder had become so overwrought, the earlier scene of Margot's return must have been even worse than expected.

'It's OK,' she explained. 'I'm not the press.' She produced

her ID. 'Remember me – Detective Sergeant Zyczynski, Thames Valley Police?'

'Oh, Lordy, yes. Sorry.' The child-minder wiped a hand on her jeans' side-pocket and seemed uncertain whether to offer it to be shaken.

'Can I come in?' Rosemary asked.

There was only a brief hesitation. 'Why not, I suppose. It's a madhouse enough already.'

Chapter Sixteen

Alice Facci had begun a run of night duty, and Nicco had assumed the coast would be clear. The worst scenario he'd expected was Violetta sleeping off heavy overnight clubbing; and she was always open to mild bribery or blackmail. However, confronted by the card tucked under the brass knocker of the front door, with its admonitory 'Night worker resting, quiet please', he knew that if he had to collect things from his own room he would need luck not to be caught. The slightest scratching of a key in the lock would alert his mother, although she could sleep through any uproar that hadn't family connections.

Her bedroom was over the front door; his own at the rear. If he crept round to the back and found something sturdy and tall enough he could shin up, cross the roof of the kitchen extension and fiddle the loose catch on his casement window. He hadn't needed to do that for three years, ever since Papa had formally presented him with a door-key on his twenty-first birthday. But then he hadn't before needed to enter the house clandestinely for fear that the police might have come seeking him there.

It went well enough until he eased himself through the window and stepped down on the sleeping cat, Serenissima, who had sought the warmth of his radiator and the convent quiet of an empty bedroom. She screamed as one hundred and forty-eight pounds landed suddenly on the root of her tail. In excruciating pain and too breathless even to retaliate, she managed to keep up a prolonged moaning until Mrs Facci, in her nightdress, came rushing through the doorway in alarm.

The open window, bringing in a blast of sub-Arctic chill, accused him. 'I was trying not to wake you,' Nicco begged in excuse.

Alice leant across the distressed cat and slammed the casement shut. 'Try harder next time,' she said scornfully. 'What have you done to Serenissima?'

'I trod on her. It was an accident.' Why must his mother always make him feel eight years old?

'Fetch the cat basket. You'll have to take her to the vet.'

'She can't be all that badly hurt, Mum.'

'How do you know? Are you going to risk feeling her all over? Even I wouldn't dare, the way she is. Do as I say.'

It would waste all his morning, sitting there in the waiting room with all those stinky animals, and even if the police were casual about such wild accusations, they would surely by then have got round to booking Margot's complaint. If he hung around he could be arrested, charged, hauled into court, found guilty of assault, even – if she went so far – entered on the Sex Offenders register.

It all depended on how long Margot's flare of fury had lasted; whether she would countenance the publicity implicit in levelling a charge against him. But then why should she? It wasn't as if he hadn't taken her before, almost as violently. In the mood she was in then, she'd wanted it rough. He'd only gone that little bit further. The police could surely be made to see it was only in play, and the woman wasn't a fragile virgin: anyone who knew her would back him on that.

And here he was being sent off on a kid's errand with the bloody cat; but it was useless appealing to his mother when she was outraged like this. Nothing would convince her as being more urgent than the relief of pain. And now that he and his sister were adults, wasn't the fucking cat her precious, adorable baby?

He would have to do as she demanded, load the now spitting feline into the wire-mesh cat basket, together with whatever of his own things he could cram in behind, then leave the house instantly.

'Go back to bed, Mum,' he pleaded. 'I'll see to it all.'

He coped, picking up some vicious scratches which he could feel bleeding into his shirtsleeves before the carrier held the satanic beast safely confined. He had left his car parked fifty yards away, near the bus stop. It was there that he risked emptying out the spitfire while scooping back his belongings in the unlikely container, ever conscious of the small crowd's hostile curiosity as they queued for the 362.

Humiliated, he slammed himself into the car, hopeful that no gossiping neighbour had been on hand to carry back the story to his parents. He assumed the cat would eventually stagger homewards or, preferably, drag itself off to some quiet corner to die.

Whichever, there would be hell to pay when he next saw his mother, but compared with all that had happened in the last few days, what did losing one foul-tempered scrap of fur and bones really matter? You needed a sense of proportion. He was a man in a man's world, had been promised promotion, shagged a celebrity woman, almost seen her husband kill himself, got a bit overexcited with her, suffered a momentary rejection, and might even now be the subject of a police inquiry.

Given the worst scenario, trouble threatened from three directions. And even when Margot had cooled down, would she be turning back to him for more of the same, or would she get vicious and damage his chances back at the studios? He knew the sort of tongue-lashing she was capable of. Everyone would accept her version of whatever story she chose to put out.

Women were the very devil. You couldn't reason out how they might react.

Thank God men were more predictable: Jolyon, for example. It was a great stroke of luck that he'd finally tired of the rural squelch of their present mooring and successfully negotiated a swap to one considerably more upmarket. Last week he'd taken on board adequate fuel, tuned up the old engine and was now set for their spending the next couple of evenings chugging up to the new mooring at Little Venice. Proximity to the well-heeled Regent's Park residential area and easier reach of his Chambers in London's Gray's Inn were extra advantages. They'd provide, he'd said, a classier choice of girls to pick up, and he'd put himself over as a budding legal eagle and a water gypsy besides. He'd made it no secret that he saw Nicco having little part in all this. He had served his purpose in sharing expenses and introducing the occasional wannabe TV actress, but that was behind him now.

Well, Jolyon could think again. Nicco was not for being grown-out-of and sloughed off; especially now, when he needed a new address. He would be claiming every right in his half-share of the narrowboat. Because he could never go and live at home again.

Margot had agreed to come in again for questioning, but only after arranging with the insurance company for a replacement Audi of the same colour, and visiting the beauty parlour for new hairstyling and professional make-up to hide the marks of Nicco's flash temper. She was still furious with him, but there were other more pressing considerations.

She chose her outfit with care, unlike her usual indifference to how she came across. This interview was important. She was going to keep a low profile, commit herself to admitting as little as possible. On it depended how the press would interpret Superintendent Yeadings' appreciation of the sorrowing widow. She had her reputation to consider; her rising career.

Widow, a strange word. And that's what she was now: perhaps not actually sorrowing, but certainly *shattered*. Who would have believed Oliver had it in him to make such a desperate bid for attention? But then, of late she had scarcely known her husband properly. He had kept too much secretly inside. After all these increasingly dreary years of living alongside him, he had surprised her. Until that revelation in their hallway as Frobisher took his departure, she had never guessed at their clandestine relationship.

Oliver a poofter; only you had to be careful what you called them nowadays. Oliver and sex, of whatever predilection, didn't seem possible somehow. And Frobisher: a doctor, you'd think he'd know better; hygienically, if for no other reason. Well, he was a bachelor, of course: had to keep some kind of interest going.

However, returning to the choice of outfit: black, of course. The short chiffon frock was lovely, but she turned it down for the calf-length gored velvet skirt with matching bolero worn with a white organza shirt. She toyed with the notion of a small, veiled hat, but that was not her. She had picked up that Yeadings could be surprisingly astute under that heavy-browed stolidity. He'd accept her better as she was, bearing up under the scandal of Oliver's suicide with dignity and little show of grief.

In the cheval mirror she approved the reflection until it struck her she resembled her mother, consulted her watch and saw she was already twenty minutes late. But he was a senior policeman, so wouldn't be in a hurry.

DS Rosemary Zyczynski was allocated to escort Mrs Charrington to interview room 2, where she waited twelve minutes before the superintendent joined her to sit with Z across the narrow table. She was offered tea or a glass of water and refused both. Last time, in his office, he had poured her filter coffee himself. The difference was disappointing, but she wasn't alarmed. It was a relief that they hadn't set a tape in their recording equipment.

'You might like to see this,' Yeadings said, opening a folder and handing across a single 8 x 10 glossy photograph.

For a hideous moment she expected a picture of Oliver, dead on the studio floor, but it was only a crumpled mass of blackened metal. Yet this was somehow far worse. It was all that remained of the car she'd bought so proudly; had delighted in driving. It felt like a stab of real, physical injury. Suppose she'd been in it, driving, when the car crashed!

'That's awful,' she said flatly. He made no reply and she felt compelled to fill the silence. 'So much has happened... just lately. It's...distressing.'

'I am so sorry for your loss,' he said.

She wasn't sure what he meant her to understand by that. Which loss – the car or her husband? Cautiously, she murmured, 'Widow is a horrible word. I hadn't realised.'

'You have our sympathy,' Yeadings assured her. 'And we intend to do all we can to look into the circumstances of what happened.'

'I thought you were satisfied that it was suicide.' Too late she regretted the word 'satisfied', but he appeared not to take it amiss.

'Is that what you think happened?'

'Oh, without question. Oliver got so easily...depressed.'

'So had he made any attempt on his life before this? Or spoken of any intention to do so?'

She frowned. 'Not to my knowledge. But there must be

a whole file on his mental condition. I mean, he'd been attending a clinic for years. One in particular, run by Toby Frobisher. His consulting rooms are in West London. He's bound to know whatever it was that finally sent Oliver over the edge.'

Again an unfortunate choice of words. She must take more time to think before answering this man's questions. Without seeming to, he was somehow pushing her, and she was determined to stay in control.

'In fact…' She paused, looking warily ahead to where this might lead her.

'Yes?'

'I believe he was a contributory factor.'

'*He?* Do you mean your husband's psychotherapist?'

'They were lovers. I'd only recently discovered that. I was going to tell him he wasn't welcome in our home anymore. Frobisher, I mean.'

Not by a flicker did the superintendent's expression change. 'And did you tell him?'

She thought for a moment. The image was clouded with remembered anger. 'Well, actually, it was Oliver I told, after he'd left; not Frobisher. But I knew he would pass it on.'

Yeadings fell silent again. Margot was conscious that the room was very small and cramped. She was wearing too many clothes. Her right hand moved to loosen the neck of her blouse. A faceted glass button fell off and rolled across the narrow table. Z stretched to trap it and pass it back.

The senior detective appeared not to notice. 'And has

the good doctor been to visit you since your husband's death?'

'No.'

'He made no offer to assist with bereavement counselling?'

'I wouldn't want that. Especially from him.'

'I can understand that. And you were intending to start divorce proceedings.'

It caught Margot by surprise. 'W-Why should you think that?'

'Because you consulted a lawyer to enquire how to initiate it.'

Apprehension struck her like a blow. Momentarily, she was breathless. How could he guess so much? Or else he'd been prying into her private life.

She had only contacted the solicitor once, and never mentioned it to any third party. This policeman had accessed private communication, made the lawyer breach rules of professional discretion. But how had he known who to approach?

As she watched narrow-eyed, Yeadings produced a slim mobile phone. She recognised it was hers, the one she'd mislaid two or three days back, possibly at the narrowboat. She held out a peremptory hand, but he withdrew his own.

'That's mine,' she claimed. 'I need it back.'

'But first it's required as evidence in an ongoing police inquiry.'

'I don't understand. What inquiry?'

'Into your husband's death, Mrs Charrington. He was

the last person to handle this phone, shortly before he fell to his death. After you mislaid it, the phone was handed to him so that he could return it to you; with tragic consequences.'

Yeadings turned it between his fingers. 'As you can see, it is quite badly damaged. We believe he did this. But fortunately we have been able to recover the voicemail in it. Shall I play it to you?'

'You have no right... I mean, those were private conversations between myself and my colleagues. There is nothing there that is relevant to my husband at all.'

'Perhaps there are calls received after you mislaid the phone: ones you've yet to hear.'

'If so, I would prefer to hear them by myself, in private. Surely I don't have to remind you, Superintendent, of Human Rights law?' She recognised the virago in her own voice, but it was too late. Yeadings' face betrayed no unease. She had reacted exactly as he'd expected.

She retreated huffily. 'Oh, do as you like. If Oliver chose to make use of the thing, that's his business, not mine.'

'He didn't send any messages, not verbal ones anyway. But perhaps his actions were a reply of sorts.'

'I don't understand.'

'Then let me help you.' There was a soft click and a half-familiar voice came through. It was her husband's solicitor, as formal and stiff as she remembered him from some past financial deal he'd brokered. But the message was primarily directed at her, not Oliver.

'Shall I repeat it?' Yeadings offered, seeing her frown. They heard the solicitor's message through again.

'You had just been in touch with his junior partner, who overlooked the possible conflict of interests, and had agreed to help with an application for divorce. This could have been challenged by the senior partner, who found it unacceptable.'

Margot sat on, struck dumb.

'Am I right?'

Then, 'But legal, surely,' she countered. 'And, anyway, I had grounds enough for a watertight case. I've already told you, how Frobisher and my precious husband were lovers.'

'Whether that was so or not, there could have followed even greater shock for your husband than the threat of divorce. There is a second piece of voicemail you should hear.'

Again the soft click, and this time it was Nicco's voice, whispering seductively, 'This is you-know-who…'

Margot sat frozen as the lascivious message poured out, all meant so beguilingly, but made obscene by outsiders eavesdropping. In detail he lingered over how he would enjoy her; she enjoy him; how they would repeat the ecstasies of their earlier love-making. Tonight, he promised, would be the experience of a lifetime. She should leave her car behind at the studios and he would bear her off to…

'No!' she shouted. 'Shut it off!' She had risen from her chair, fists balled, furious.

'Mrs Charrington, please sit down. Perhaps you should explain what all that was about.'

She sank back, covering her face.

'Let me help you remember. On Friday evening, at the close of your shoot, you left your car behind at the studios,

217

as so many wisely did after the celebration party. And it was from there that it was stolen, later found burnt out, with the body of an unknown woman hidden in the boot.

'We need you to help us understand what else happened. Did you follow the phoned invitation and leave in this young man's car – immediately after your husband had fallen from the grid?'

Chapter Seventeen

Margot had resorted to tears. One or two of them, Yeadings thought, could have been genuine: for her predicament, rather than from grief. But she was still a single-breasted Amazon.

Z repeated the offer of tea, coffee, a glass of water. This time Margot accepted. It would give her time to decide how much she was obliged to admit to.

'I was in shock,' she said after the necessary pause, hugging the plastic beaker of tea with both hands. 'I still am; can't think straight.'

'You needed someone to talk to, who would understand,' Yeadings suggested softly.

'I couldn't go home...the children, my mother. How could I explain to them about Oliver?'

'They were shocked too when they learnt he was dead. And then you disappeared, which was an added worry.'

'I rang to explain I was with friends.'

Yeadings let a little silence build, then, 'How did you receive your injuries?' he pursued on a new tack.

Margot put a hand to her face, shocked that he'd

penetrated the make-up. 'It was on the boat. It rocks when another one goes by, and I stumbled. The canal's narrow down by the lock. I went there because it's peaceful. I had so much to work out in my mind.'

She was talking faster, almost breathless in panic. No way would she admit that that despicable young cameraman had abused her.

'You were punched, weren't you?' Zyczynski said, on a nod from the Boss. 'It was Niccolo Facci who attacked you – his boat you were staying on. Why should he do that?'

Margot tried to force her hands to stop shaking. They already knew too much. Had they dragged Nicco in and he'd confessed?

'Do you intend to charge him with Actual Bodily Harm?' Yeadings enquired before she could answer.

'I – I… No. It was my fault. I'd just spilt hot coffee on him. He's quick to react. Just a flash of temper. He was sorry straight after,' she lied. 'Didn't he tell you?'

'Not in exactly the same words.' That was strictly true, but Yeadings wondered what version of the incident they would get out of him once he was brought in. For the moment he was missing, as was the fuchsia-painted narrowboat he'd been living on. Enquiries at Denham lock had revealed it had not passed through. That meant the vessel must have reversed, in order to turn at some wider point and start chugging on towards London. It would hardly take a high-speed chase to follow it up. But it would already be in the Met's zone of operations.

Margot took a deep breath, 'Look, Superintendent, none of this has anything to do with what happened to my car. Have you made any progress in tracing who took it? Or whose body was found in the wreck?'

'We are following a definite line of inquiry,' he told her, totally stolid Plod. 'You will be informed when the investigation is complete. Meanwhile, I must ask you to stay at whatever address you will now give my sergeant, and certainly not leave the Thames Valley area without informing her beforehand. You are free to go then.'

No thanks for my having troubled to come in, she thought bitterly, scribbling on the notepad Z pushed across. But at least he hadn't demanded her passport. Anyone would have thought from his final tone that she was some kind of suspect herself. It was galling, though, that if she required an alibi for anything that had occurred during that Friday-Saturday night, the only person who could supply it was Nicco.

'You have the address already. I shall be at my home.' She stood up stiffly, smoothed her velvet skirt and walked out.

'Well?' Yeadings demanded of DC Silver, who accosted him in reception as he was passing through. 'What has CCTV revealed?'

'Several brief sightings of the Audi early on, but nothing once it entered minor roads, sir. Only there's something else that might be important. I've been checking at garages for petrol supplied in cans during that night, because I don't think the torching was premeditated mischief by kids. Someone suddenly had to get hold of an accelerant because he needed to dispose of the body. Not many people keep a store ready for occasions like that.'

'Seems reasonable. Lead on, then.' He followed Silver towards the CID office and Z fell in behind.

'There were two cans filled at pumps on Friday night at Tesco in Old Amersham; one on Saturday night at the Bulstrode, Gerrards Cross, and two farther out which seem less likely for our guy under pressure. I've run the tapes together, sir.'

They gathered round the screen. 'Here's Tesco's fuel forecourt on Friday night. Both male drivers, one with a female passenger. A blue Mazda, then a silver Nissan Micra. Both men paid at the pump by credit card. One was fairly recognisable, the other muffled under a flat cap. It was snowing slightly at the time. No glimpse of the Audi Cabriolet anywhere.'

'The second man's elderly,' Z murmured. 'And the woman passenger in the first car's a possible witness. Neither a very likely arsonist. Especially using a card to pay.'

'Then there's this one,' Silver offered, tapping the keyboard. 'At the Bulstrode Garage, a hoodie, dressed in navy or black, which seems promising. He had to buy a can as well, but he's on foot. On the other hand, the garage is on the direct route for Fulmer/Stoke Poges. You'd turn off the A40 at the French Horn pub.'

He grinned up at the Boss. 'So I got hold of the pub's car park CCTV tape and caught him a few minutes later flashing by on a bike. He took the right turn.'

'Could be an innocent, ran out of gas, dumped the bike and had to walk back for fuel,' Z discouraged him.

'Chose to ride past a well-lit garage and walk back? I don't think so,' Yeadings argued.

'I know it's the Audi we're looking for,' Silver allowed, 'but I tried enhancing the shot. The bike's not entirely irrelevant. It's a Kawasaki Ninja. I got the two final letters on the rear licence plate, and I'm not dead certain the rider was a man. It could have been a girl: someone young and wiry, in any case. So I checked, and those two letters I picked up are ones we've already recorded.'

'On Jenny Barnes's bike?' Z breathed. 'You think it could be her?'

'That's stretching a coincidence;' Yeadings cautioned, 'but it's the best guess we've got so far. Let's go with it until proved wrong. Athene doubted she'd have gone with Jamie on his walking tour. She could still be around locally, keeping a low profile.'

Two figures had moved in behind as they bent over the screen. 'DI Salmon, get up to Notting Hill and see if she's back home,' Mott ordered the other.

He turned to Yeadings. 'It's still vital we check with Jamie whether Jenny's with him. As floor manager, he struck me as a damn sight more organised than his scruffy gear suggests. He'd surely have collected maps and made a route plan for the tour. They could be on his home computer. Silver, you have his address. Get over there and ask around where he's gone. If we can contact local police up north there's a slim chance of discovering where Jenny might be.'

'With a search warrant, sir, to access his hard drive?'

Yeadings grunted. 'Not a chance. We've nothing to

223

persuade a magistrate that the man's remotely involved in a murder. Use your initiative to wheedle your way in.'

Mott leant over the computer and clicked on an icon. 'He rents an upper flat from an elderly relative who lives on the ground floor. Get on to her right away, Silver. And award yourself a Brownie point for picking up on the bike.'

He turned to Zyczynski. 'I want you, Z, to go along with DI Salmon. He'll have to warn the Met he's making enquiries on their patch.'

She nodded. Smooth things over, he meant, in case the Salmon started swimming against the current.

'If you find Jenny Barnes at home, show interest in her bike. It might reveal something useful.'

Zyczynski grinned. 'Right, guv. I'll take the ladette line of sheer envy.'

'OK, then. Scatter. What's holding you all back?'

The man lay on in the tub, staring at the bathroom's purple ceiling studded with gilt stars, until the water began to cool. The rest of the flat's décor was pretty cool too, he thought: a bit harem-style with those floaty sheer drapes in psychedelic colours. He ran the hot tap until the water was steaming again.

Paradiso was a bath essence he hadn't heard of, but it was well suited to his present mood: maybe a tad too girly, but then he was taking her place, wasn't he? He wondered if he might get round to using the tinted shampoo from her bathroom cupboard, and see how well it would 'illuminate the red highlights' as claimed on the box. It wasn't an out-

and-out dye, but he still felt let-down that her red hair had proved less than one hundred per cent natural.

It was one of a number of small disappointments that moving in here had provided, but so far he'd managed to forgive her. The most puzzling were the two messages left on her answer-phone: a gravel-voiced man complaining about her failure to 'make the pick-up'; and then, a second time, about not having forwarded 'the necessary'. These had been delivered with increasing annoyance, and he'd taken strong exception to the man's presumption. Later, as he listened to its third message prompt on Jenny's flip recording – 'I'm out, darlings. Feel free to leave a message after the tone' – the man had been back, openly livid, demanding she ring instantly on her return.

That was when, in fury, he'd torn out the phone cable, picked up the bloody machine and hurled it against the wall. If the man had been there in person that was the least he'd have suffered.

Startling him now from his musings in the water, a bell rang shrilly. Someone down at the street door was demanding to be let in. He knew it couldn't be Jenny, and anyway, she'd have had her keys. He heaved himself on his elbows to listen. A short pause and then a second, prolonged ring: some uncouth git keeping his finger on the button.

It was pleasant to keep the loser waiting. He'd no intention of stirring, unless, of course, there was an attack on the newly fixed front door and someone attempted to get upstairs. Tonight he'd remove the light bulb and fix a booby trap. She should have had protection of that sort already. She had only to have asked him, admitted how vulnerable she was, and he'd have happily constructed something fool-proof to keep her safe, just in case. It was the sort of thing he was good at.

At street level, DI Salmon and the Met constable assigned to keep an eye on him stood back to scan the upstairs windows. Despite the heavily overcast sky, no lights showed. There was no curtain-twitching. Salmon gave up. 'I'll give you a lift back,' he said shortly. It sounded more of a threat than an invitation.

'No need,' said the beat officer. 'I'll take a look round the back and then continue on foot patrol.'

'Hey, Z, we're going,' the DI shouted, as she hesitated by the door to the picture framer's.

'Hang on a sec.' A shop bell pinged as she went in. The elderly owner appeared from behind a curtain of minute wooden plaques mounted on gilt cords and separated by small golden beads. It jingled as it moved and his voice was pitched close in the same octave. 'Good evening. How can I help you?'

Z explained that she'd hoped to visit her friend Jenny upstairs, and could leave no message because the letterbox appeared to be blocked up from the inside.

'Really? Are you sure?'

'She's probably fixed a draught excluder.'

'Oh, I see. Well, you're welcome to leave a note with me. I'll let her have it when she returns. Actually, I haven't seen her since Friday morning, when she left for work.'

He waved her to a small rosewood table and produced

a trade circular with the shop's heading: *Duncan Rennie, Fine Art Dealer, Restoration and Picture Framing.* Z bent to scribble a note. 'I don't suppose you would know where she's gone, or for how long, Mr Rennie?'

'I'm afraid not. Naturally, as an independent young woman, as you are yourself, she has her own interests. As, for that matter, do I. But I believe she was finishing a project at the studios this past week. Perhaps she's gone for a short break on her bike.'

He frowned. 'But I wish she'd thought to cancel her milk delivery. It's not like her to be forgetful. I take it in for her, you see. Now I have a small milk lake to dispose of. I don't suppose you would care to...? No, of course not.'

Z smiled, folded the note over, handed it to him with her thanks and went to rejoin the impatient Salmon in his car.

'Let's hope Silver's been more fortunate at the other place,' he growled, as she belted herself in.

Miss Beatrice Shelby thought what a nice boy young Mr Silver was. And so well turned out. Not like her nephew Jamie, who wore an odd assortment of clothes and sometimes brought loud young women home after she'd retired for the night. Still, he never kept her waiting for the rent and seemed to hold down a well-paid job over in Maidenhead at some television company.

When next she wrote to her married sister in New Zealand, she'd be sure to say what a pleasant young man he had for a friend, and a policeman too, such a responsible job in these lawless days.

It seemed Mr Silver needed to consult some maps Jamie had used for his walking tour. She accompanied him upstairs, unlocked the door to his flat and helped the young man search through the three shelves of books – some of them with such lurid covers – in his sitting room.

While she went down to make tea and set out her best china, Silver booted up Jamie's computer and took off the information he required. 'Piece of cake,' he told himself, dropped the latch and joined Miss Selby downstairs over Earl Gray tea and home-baked muffins.

Duncan Rennie despatched his next customer with a wrapped 16 x 20 canvas of a mock Holbein portrait, and observed as the doorbell tinkled for the man's departure that there was no sign yet of the expected delivery of timber: time perhaps to pop out to the kitchen and start up his cappuccino machine.

It was as he carefully measured out Lavazza filter coffee that he heard the unmistakable sound of bathwater flushing down from Jenny's flat above.

That would explain why her friend had been unable to get an answer at the door. Naturally, Jenny wouldn't have rushed to open up in a wet and unclothed state. It could have been a stranger ringing.

The young lady visitor had written her mobile number on the outside of the note for Jenny. Maybe if he rang her straight away she could turn back and be saved a lost journey. But perhaps he shouldn't contact her before he'd warned Jenny who it was. And in any case, his throat was dry from dealing with the previous hard-to-persuade customer. His need for caffeine came first.

Later he would turn the *Closed* sign on the door and trot up to have a word with Jenny.

In the dim candlelit gloom, he sat staring into the full-length mirror. His hair was almost the right length. If he trimmed it a bit behind the ears and sleeked two streaks forward below the cheekbones it really gave the look of her, now that he'd used twice the amount of tint the packet had suggested.

Him a redhead. How his brother would have laughed. No, for once he'd have been impressed.

Farther down, the reflection wasn't good. He'd need to cover the chest, roll up some tights to use as stuffing – not that she was a busty female, but his own skinny ribs wouldn't fool a blind beggar.

In her wardrobe there were dresses as well as the usual jeans and T-shirts she'd worn to work. He would let them work their magic on him, already seduced by the scents and colours of her home.

Still facing the mirror, he balanced her make-up kit on knees held tight together like girls did. He'd need quite a bit to cover up his sallow skin, produce the perfect English Rose. For blusher there was a range of either orangey pink or mauvish pink, with plenty of dark eyeliners; and lipsticks that ranged from scarlet to crimson-black. Choice must depend on which dress he went for. He closed his eyes to recall the contents of the wardrobe. It would need to be something that felt good against the skin, one of those silky fabrics he'd run through his fingers and that still carried the magical scent of her.

Lilac; wasn't that what they called that pale purple? And the long evening dress had thin straps covered in diamante studs. Glitzy: that was Jenny at night. No; it was more than that. It was *him*.

The reflection was enchanting. Consumed by ardour, he leant slowly forward to press his lips on the cool surface of the mirror.

Chapter Eighteen

Margot managed not to slam the phone down, swearing only after she had firmly replaced it on a chilly 'Goodnight, Roger.' What did the fool of a man expect her to do? He'd had his chance and blown it. A lacklustre performance throughout the series couldn't be salvaged by briefly appearing *simpatico* at the end. As station officer, he had been killed off; he must look for work elsewhere. The company lawyers had assured Greg the man's contract wasn't breached, it had simply lapsed.

And then this demand to know Jenny's address; as though Margot carried a directory around with her! She'd compromised by reading the girl's mobile number off the phone notepad. Let him risk ringing her and see how pleased she'd be to have her free time disturbed. And why did he need to contact the girl? Surely he didn't imagine Margot's assistant had the influence to reverse a decision already approved by her superiors?

She ran a hand through her hair. She didn't need this pointless bother. Too much was piling up on her, and everything she'd thought permanent was falling apart.

Now there were all the funeral arrangements to make; caterers to select; service sheets to set up and order at the printer's; personal invitations to dispatch. And still the police had given no firm date for when the body could be released. She'd be launched on rehearsals for the next series of *All Fired Up* before she was clear of this wretched business.

Carlotta had insisted that any public reference to Oliver's scandalous end would be in utterly bad taste, but Mother still lived in the past. Suicide wasn't the shocking matter it had been in her younger days, and the vulture press had already been dipping their bloody beaks in it. Nowadays, anything dodgy about a well-known figure was considered newsworthy.

She should really settle to dealing with the clutter of funeral chores. First, choose the order of cremation, and then a separate memorial service at the Actors' Church of St Paul in Covent Garden; this to be a celebrity occasion with all the big television and stage names turning up. Obviously, the Savoy for a reception afterwards. So much to organise!

And then, on top of all this extra work, Charlie had chosen to play up at school and attack another little boy with a chair, actually breaking a leg off it and drawing blood from the boy. Or so the teacher had reported.

'He's upset and insecure,' Joanna tried to excuse him. 'He was very fond of his daddy. He feels suddenly alone and he's scared of what might happen to the rest of us. He wakes up sobbing and won't be comforted.'

'You must deal with it,' Margot had retorted, 'and

explain to his headmistress I cannot possibly come and see her at a time like this. It was only a *chair* leg that came off, for God's sake, not the child's. Charlie was probably provoked. It shows he's started to stand up for himself.'

'Fucking harpy!' Roger ground out, slamming the phone down. Like a ruddy tank, Margot had rolled right over him and missed what he was really after: hunting for Jenny. How could she ever understand his desperate situation? Not that he dared explain.

It had to be Jenny. How could he risk being seen hanging around sleazy alleys, accosting dubious strangers to supply his needs? Thanks to the programme's improved ratings, he was recognised now wherever he went, and God only knew what the outcome could be if he contacted criminals who packed knives and guns.

Every day you could read in the papers how rife the traffic was, with lowlifes dealing openly at every street corner; waiting outside schools to snare the kids. But where were they when your supplier had walked out on you, and you were mad to get a fix?

Jenny couldn't just disappear! Didn't the fool of a girl realise what a hole she'd left him in – and it was all of her doing, getting him on that final high. Maybe it was deliberate, to ensure he stayed dependent.

All I need is something to keep going, until I can get the habit to tail off. I'm not addicted; nothing serious like that!

He plunged his head into his hands, trying to remember the sequence in which things had happened on that last day at the studios. Margot had come to the gallery window, scowling down on the set, doing her silent-bitch thing, with her mouth a thin, straight line. She'd ordered a break and Jenny had been sent to work him over. But there was a pause before the girl appeared to haul him off somewhere quiet and hand over the stuff he needed.

He was sure Margot knew nothing of Jenny's sideline. It was lucky that the girl had had the stuff handy to get him through those final bloody scenes. But where had she fetched it from? A secret stash somewhere in the building that only she had access to? Not her locker – too incriminating, and the girl wasn't stupid. So where? Some place that didn't lead back to her, in case it was ever discovered? No, it would be hidden in a spot that implicated someone else, yet wasn't regularly examined.

He felt excitement rising at his cleverness in working through her probable precautions. He was surely on the right track So, go a little further, try to recall her movements later when they were all packing up. She'd have wanted to secure any stock left over, to take it away when she left.

But suddenly, at the end of the shoot, before all the techs had finished clearing away, all hell had broken loose when Oliver Charrington jumped – or fell – from the grid, where he shouldn't have been anyway. After that, everything was a blur.

Roger hadn't seen it happen. As a member of the cast, he'd already started on the party when people started yelling and running all over the place. And then the police swarmed in to sort everyone into groups and make them answer questions.

So where was Jenny in all this? Did she have time to recover the rest of her stash? She had to make sure nothing was left behind because the studios were heavily booked, and the pop video lot were due to take over the next day. But, with the police controlling all movement and taping off the whole performance area, she wouldn't have been able to move around freely. Nor would she have kept anything on her once they took over, in case they had sniffer dogs with them. So perhaps that meant that what he needed was still there, hidden, wherever she'd kept it. In the area taped off?

The grid, where Charrington fell from! That was where they'd been most busy; that and the spot where the poor devil had landed. But, earlier, when Jenny had gone to fetch his fix, there hadn't been time for her to climb as far as the grid itself. Somewhere on the way, then? Anywhere, in fact, behind the cyc; the stuff could be concealed in one of those unused junction boxes set into the walls.

That was clever, because if ever Telehouse security had happened on the crack, their natural suspect for a dealer would be the lighting gaffer who was allowed back there to check on his hoists in the grid. That was Barry Farlow, poor sod. Except that he'd gone sick that last week, and his assistant had taken over, the sulky weirdo called Carl something. Whitsett, was it? No; Winslow: The Winslow Boy, as in the play and film of that name. Not that he'd have known of Jenny's stash. He would simply have featured as the likely fall guy.

It was good, all these details coming back to him. It showed he was getting a grip on himself.

By now the police should have finished at Telehouse. According to today's *Telegraph*, Charrington's death was being accepted as suicide. Anything they still needed to poke into would be in his home area.

Luckily, due to so much upset at the time, security had let him leave without surrendering his visitor's pass. He could still get in by the props entrance, mix in with the new video crowd, and hunt for what Jenny hadn't had time to recover. That would have to tide him over until she got in touch again.

Duncan Rennie rinsed his coffee cup under the tap and left it upturned with its saucer on the draining board. He examined himself in the small mirror over the sink and smoothed his white hair. He decided he'd look a lot younger without his gold-rimmed spectacles and removed them, carefully folding them in their case on the corner of the cash register where he'd not have to blunder about to find them.

Foolish old fellow, he accused himself. As if a pretty young woman like Jenny would even notice how he looked. Nevertheless, he straightened his tie and checked the hang of his jacket before setting off upstairs. By now she'd had time enough to get herself dressed, but not yet to have left for a night out on the town.

It probably wasn't an important message he had for her, but it always gave him a lift seeing her and being shown the latest changes she'd made to her rooms. She put so much imagination into it, had a flair for décor, even if the results were sometimes a trifle bizarre. And she always seemed pleased when they met.

The staircase was in darkness as he went up. This was the second time that week. It must be more than a faulty bulb. Tomorrow he would see about having the wiring checked. Fortunately, the doorbell wasn't affected. He heard its piercing ring, followed by the sound of something falling or being knocked over beyond the door. It took a few minutes for it to be opened and he was ready with his apology.

'Jenny, my dear, I'm so sorry. I must have startled you.'

She said nothing, just stood there staring, in a long, diaphanous gown with glittery shoulder straps, silhouetted against flickering candlelight. He could see through the flimsy material to the outline of her legs.

A door to her left was open, showing the corner of a room with a pile of bright fabrics strewn over the bed. She had been choosing an outfit, was on the point of going out, or else expecting company – someone very special, a lover perhaps – and his arrival was most ill-timed.

Embarrassed, he started on more apologies, but she reached for his jacket and pulled him roughly inside.

Something was very wrong. She seemed to tower over him, not welcoming but hostile, menacing.

'Jenny, dear—'

'*You – lecherous – old – pervert!*' she accused in a vicious growl, thrusting him back against the inner wall. A bunched fist landed in his abdomen, doubling him up. All his breath was knocked out of him. Agonising, he felt his legs give way; but she held him up against the wall with her other hand. The fist struck again and again before she let him drop to the floor. And then the kicking began, viciously aimed at head and ribs, as he curled up, sobbing, babbling for her to stop.

Losing consciousness, he imagined he saw her feet as huge, and quite bare. The relentless rhythm continued: *thud, thud, thud*, with unimaginable pain. She's killing me, he thought, and a final flash of white pain exploded into darkness.

Salmon and Z reported back that Jenny Barnes had still not returned to her flat and hadn't been seen there since the Friday morning of the final shoot at Telehouse. So far as her landlord knew, she had not returned that night and her motorcycle was not where she normally left it, in the woodshed behind his shop.

Yeadings and his DCI were in conference over it. 'All we have is this possible sighting of a biker picking up a can of petrol on Friday night,' Mott said. 'We can still eliminate Jenny for that if Cumbrian police pick her up with Jamie on his walking tour. They're alerting hostels and B&Bs along the trails Silver found the maps for, but I'm pretty sure we'll find he's travelling on his own.'

The internal phone rang. 'DCI Mott,' Angus announced, reaching for it. He listened, nodding to Yeadings that something of interest was coming through.

'Did he indeed? Thank you, Sergeant. Get a uniform to pick him up ASAP.'

He replaced the receiver and turned to the

superintendent. 'Roger Bascombe, the actor playing the station officer in *All Fired Up*, has turned up at Telehouse and refused to account to security for trying to gain entry on a cancelled pass. As we know, they change the colour regularly. His was green, and it's blue for the new group that was meant to move in today. He seemed to think the pop video shoot was still on schedule, but walked straight in on SOCO taking the place apart.'

'I suppose he's worth questioning, though I doubt there's any connection with the suicide. He was fully occupied on the set when Charrington must have gone up into the grid. And the messages found on Margot's mobile could be sufficient to account for Oliver's sudden decision to take his own life. He seemed to have been quite besotted with his wife.

'On the other hand, this actor may be able to cast some light on drug abuse among the cast and technical crew – perhaps he went there looking for the stash we found. Athene told us he'd managed to pull a rabbit out of the hat for his final performance – was that drug induced? And, rather than giving him a pep talk, did Jenny give him something a little stronger? We need to talk to him; if he is a user in search of his next hit, he might lead us to his dealer, which might bring us to the missing Jenny. Given such a choice for suspects, we need all the help we can get from any direction.'

'There's nothing fresh from forensics about the burnt body,' Mott said gloomily. 'They're trying some new restorative measures on the bone, but don't offer much chance of anything useful for an ID. And anyway, it would be six weeks at least before any results are likely to show. If only Jenny wasn't a possible as the biker who bought loose petrol, I'd have fancied her for our victim. The age range is right and she has disappeared rather thoroughly.'

Yeadings stood and went over to gaze out of the window. 'Even if the tape is further enhanced and does confirm it was her at the garage, she could still be our body. Was some accomplice – the car thief, say – waiting at the crash scene for her to return with the fuel? And what would happen then? A disagreement that came to blows? It could have ended in the girl being strangled. Then there'd be more than a crashed car to dispose of: Jenny too, conveniently removing the threat of a witness to the car snatch.'

Mott nodded. 'A deliberate act, rather than a panicky accident? It's a not uncommon scenario: a minor crime covered up by a major one.' He visualised the scene. 'Jenny was young, fit, apparently well aware of what was going on around her. It would have taken someone with considerably more strength to overpower her.'

'A man, then?'

'I would expect so. The fire has destroyed any defensive wounds or fingernail scrapings that might have helped us identify him. Forensics have been just as negative on the woman, although Prof Littlejohn has been trying for an ID by taking a dental imprint. But the teeth were almost pristine, except for that capped lower canine, and heat will have distorted the original shape of the mouth. Jenny Barnes's dentist can't help. He denies having done any capping. She had simply had polishing and hygiene treatment on her last visit eighteen months ago.'

'She could have gone elsewhere for emergency work. But let's consider another alternative,' Yeadings suggested. 'If Jenny was involved in the torching, we have a bike as well as a car to explain away. Were both involved in the collision with the tree? Had the joyrider run into the girl, knocked her off the bike, injuring her fatally, so that he had to get rid of her body? And got away on her bike, if it wasn't too badly damaged?'

'But then how could she have been the biker at the garage who fetched the petrol? Maybe there was a second female present, even a pedestrian, who got injured and ended in the burnt-out car.'

Yeadings sighed. 'Two separate vehicles from the *All Fired Up* programme being together out on that country road in the early hours? It's too coincidental. Where the crash happened is nowhere on anyone's way home from Maidenhead. That's been double-checked. Or do you see Jenny and some unknown man taking the Audi from Telehouse car park for a lark and meaning to return it before Margot would pick it up the following day? Later she'd expect to go back for the bike.'

'But with the Audi crashed, she'd have had to go back on foot. And the bike has disappeared from there as certainly as Jenny.'

'They would have taken Margot's car on Friday night. But the torching wasn't until the night of Saturday–Sunday. There was time for a lot to go awry in the meantime,' Yeadings pointed out.

'The Audi's a coupé. Why not drop the top and load the bike into the rear, under plastic sheeting or something?'

Yeadings came back to his desk and sat down. 'Angus, it would take a couple of Titans to lift the thing in. The only way to load a bike that size would be to run it up a ramp into a trade van.'

'They could have tried. I'll have lab technicians re-examine the area for oil stains of varieties not used in cars. I've never known a bike, however new, not to leave some traces when it's been manhandled.'

A little silence built while both considered the impasse they'd reached. Yeadings was the first to break it. 'If the bike was there at the burning, and the killer used it to get away, then I'm afraid we can be pretty sure who our dead woman is. Jenny wouldn't have let it go lightly.'

Chapter Nineteen

Never the greatest of dramatic actors, Roger's forte was a display of stupefied incomprehension when anyone implied he was out of line. He used it now to good effect, and the young constable sent to bring him in, persuaded that DCI Mott was barking up a whole grove of wrong trees, let him go unaccompanied for a call of nature in the security lodge.

Balanced on the lavatory seat, he hammered on the hinges of the louvred window, first with his fist until the pain was unendurable, and then with the iron bolt which he managed to extract from the door. With his damaged right hand swathed in magnolia-tinted Petal Soft toilet tissue, he heaved himself to the required height and squeezed through the narrow space, falling awkwardly to the roadside outside the lodge.

It had been drizzling again and his light grey raincoat was soaked down one side with unsavoury and chilling mud. But he was free. He limped to where he'd parked his car fifty yards along the lane and drove out of Maidenhead.

Roger joined the traffic flow on the eastbound Bath Road, darting furtive glances at his rear-view mirror for signs of pursuit; but it seemed he hadn't yet been missed. The young constable sent to fetch him had drifted across to see what a group of forensic experts were packing in their van and had got into conversation with them.

What mattered now, since finding a fix at Telehouse had proved impossible, was again to concentrate on running Jenny down. Margot couldn't – or wouldn't – help, sour old cow. That left only Jamie. He and Jenny had been close enough to share travel, and probably beds, before she acquired her Kawasaki bike and independence.

And who could afford a bike like that without her very profitable second line of business? She must have had other customers at the studios before she ever started to help him out.

Jamie would surely know where she lived. Roger couldn't think why he hadn't gone straight to him first. His Victorian terrace house, or rather his old auntie's, was on Roger's way back to his own flat. He'd often seen the old tan Nissan parked outside as he'd gone by at weekends.

'Barry Farlow?' Yeadings repeated as Beaumont phoned in the latest news to reach the CID office.

'Yessir. Just another name on the almighty long list from Telehouse that we're working through to little avail. He hasn't featured in the investigation because he wasn't present on the Friday that Oliver Charrington went overboard, so to speak. He was the lighting gaffer, but he'd gone sick earlier in the week and his number two, Carl

Winslow, was the one we interviewed.'

'Whom Athene had described as a bit of a mute,' Yeadings recalled.

'That's the guy. His contribution wasn't up to much. Well, he's not the interesting party, as it happens. It's Barry Farlow, the one who collapsed at work and went sick. He was taken to Wycombe General Hospital with a mystery illness which rapidly worsened and now he's in ITU, suspected of metallic poisoning ingested over a period. I don't see where he fits into our scheme of things, but it's interesting that here we have yet another character from the Telehouse list who could go missing any minute now, and this one permanently. Could be our body count will reach three. I just thought you should know.'

'Metallic poisoning?' Yeadings queried. 'Have they found arsenic in him, then?'

'The hospital won't yet name a specific poison. There's a chance it could have been accidental, innocently taken through something he contacted in his work. He was responsible for handling quite a bit of gear, with the heavy lighting and the electrical hoists used to lift them to the grid. On the other hand—'

'The grid,' Yeadings interrupted sharply. 'As head of lighting he'd have been authorised to check on all equipment behind the cyc, which is where SOCO turned up the supply of heroin, crack and Ecstasy. Maybe he was a user and got hold of the wrong stuff by mistake.'

'Or discovered the stash and infiltrated the chain. So did the dealer discover stuff was leaking away and substitute something to put him off for good? We're turning up some quite dodgy characters at the studios, one way and another.'

'Leave it with me,' Yeadings ordered. 'I'll get access to the man's medical notes through someone I know at the hospital. Also contact his GP.

'Meanwhile, I want you to start sniffing among the people who would have observed him over a period. It's important to know how long his health was failing and whether it had been affecting his work or home life. And, apart from that, we have to consider if he could be the dealer himself, obliged to leave his supplies behind when he collapsed and was taken to hospital.'

Athene, Beaumont decided. He would quite enjoy another session with that bright young lady. Might even suggest a meal out somewhere cosy where she'd relax and let her hair down; or take those fearsome glasses off, anyway.

Time was of the essence, and Roger was getting increasingly jumpy. He turned up the car's heating and slumped lower in the driving seat, shivering as he kept watch on the house through his wing mirror. Why didn't the old girl decide to slip out to the corner shop, visit a friend or a bingo hall: anything to give him a chance to break in and look through Jamie's stuff.

He knew she was there because the downstairs lights were on and he'd seen her shadow move across the closed curtains of the front room. When the light went out there he hoped she'd decided on an early night, but no such luck. He'd waited an interminable fifteen minutes and then stolen round by the side gate to peep in at the rear. She was now seated at the kitchen table sticking labels on a number of Kilner jars containing pickled onions or beetroot while occasionally glancing across at a small TV on the opposite wall.

He moved back and stared up at Jamie's windows. No handy ivy-cladding or ancient wisteria trunks; this place was unadorned brickwork, plain as a municipal public loo. There was a drainpipe running from the gutter at one end of the roof and ending in a battered water butt. If he carried across one of the metal chairs on the patio, he thought he could climb up and get a purchase on the pipe.

Careful to keep all noise below the TV volume seeping from the house, he set up the preparations. The chair wobbled on uneven flagstones as he mounted it. The water butt's lid of slatted wood had a chunk missing and threatened to tip in. He kept it flat by crawling onto it, belly down, and ran an exploratory hand over the pipe to test its soundness. With a dull, grating sound the lowest bracket came away from the wall. It was useless. He tried to slide back down onto the chair but the butt's lid upended and drenched him with stale rainwater. God, this was getting as farcical as the rubbish script of *All Fired Up*, except that there he'd have had access to stout, extending ladders and a stand-in to do all the necessary scrambling.

There was nothing for it. He'd have to go round to the front again, ring the bloody doorbell and think up some story that would gain him entry to Jamie's flat. A pity he wasn't in his fireman's uniform so he could demand to check on her safety measures for the house.

As he came within feet of the front door a brilliant spotlight picked him out. In his present state he could have done with a little obscurity, but he put his faith in elderly eyes not being sharp enough to pick up the soakings he'd endured.

A minute elapsed before he rang again. Then a soft-slipper shuffle was followed by the sound of a chain being carefully slotted into place, and the door yielded by two inches.

'Can't you read the notice?' a tetchy old voice demanded.

He saw it then, the plastic-coated form handed out by the police, prohibiting selling and buying at the door. It was glued to the door jamb at shoulder level.

'No hawkers!'

'I'm not a hawker.'

'I don't care what you are. I don't open up for strangers after dark.'

'But I'm a friend of Jamie's, a colleague on the telly show he's been recording. My name's Roger. He must have mentioned me. I'm an actor. I play the boss at the fire station.'

'The one in the white helmet?'

'How did you know?'

'He showed me some still shots.' She didn't sound impressed.

'Look, Mrs—'

'It's *Miss*,' she corrected severely. 'Miss Beatrice Shelby. I'm Jamie's aunt.'

'Yes, I know. He's often mentioned you,' Roger lied desperately.

It seemed to mollify her somewhat. 'Well, what are you wanting at this time of night? My nephew's away.'

'I'm in a bit of a hole. I lent him a book, you see. It was from the library and it has to go back by tomorrow. And that's when I go away for a month. Abroad.' He was inventing wildly. 'To New York. I've been offered a big part there in a Broadway production.'

The richness of detail was clearly having an accumulative effect. Or perhaps the criminal implication of a library book's late return weighed heavily in the balance. Miss Shelby was famously law-abiding.

'Well…it's a nuisance, but just a minute.'

The door slammed in his face and the chain rattled again. When she opened up she still looked doubtful.

'You're wise to take precautions,' he babbled. 'You do hear of such awful things happening.'

That wasn't the best reminder for a nervous elderly lady on her own. Her mouth trembled. She had time now to take in his whole appearance, and there was a strange smell coming off him, like stagnant ditches or rotting leaves in a compost bin. He seemed to have been standing for some time in the rain. Without a proper hat or umbrella.

'What was it called?' she summoned the wit to demand, having some idea that she could go upstairs and get the book, while he waited outside on the doorstep.

'Eh?'

'The library book.'

'Oh my God, what *was* it called? I clean forget the title,

249

but I'd know it by the cover. It's about global warming.'

Not a very nice person, she observed. He blasphemed. Of course younger people did use swear words nowadays. It went with his trampish appearance and impatient manner – and she recalled Jamie hadn't had a great opinion of him as an actor.

'Look, I won't be a jiffy. It'll be sitting right there on his bookshelf.' He had edged past her as she ruminated, and now was at the foot of the stairs. She was helpless to stop him.

He went up two at a time, his left hand squeaking stickily as he grabbed at the banister rail. The other hand was wrapped in something that looked like stained pink tissues. A most peculiar man altogether.

He passed out of sight, and she knew at once what to do. That other young man, the nice friend of Jamie's who called before, had left his card with her. And he was a policeman. He'd tell her how to deal with this unpleasant, pushy person. She could ring him, and then somebody would know. Just in case something nasty did happen to her.

DC Silver observed Beaumont's departure and rejoiced that he wasn't the one to be tasked. As soon as he'd cleared up here he could get off home. He had just extracted his report from the printer and was correcting by hand the few typos that had crept in, mostly due to missing vowels. His fingers still fumbled on the far right end of the keyboard since he'd had to land a few punches during an affray attended with uniform. The errors didn't worry him, secure in his acceptance as the team's IT wizard.

His mobile sang out a phrase from Holst's 'Jupiter'. He flipped it open, but didn't recognise the number on the screen. This was a new one. He keyed the receive button and an excited elderly female voice answered his 'DC Silver, Thames Valley Police.'

He knew at once who it was. 'Miss Shelby,' he interrupted, to slow her down. 'What can I do for you?'

She poured out the tale: Jamie away – well, of course he knew that – and a quite peculiar man was trying to get into his rooms. She knew she shouldn't have opened the door to him but he'd claimed to be one of the actors from the TV series at Jamie's studios. He'd just pushed past her into the hall – so rude! – and she didn't dare go up there after him. It sounded like he was trying to force the door, throwing himself against it and...

'Miss Shelby, I'm on my way. Can you go to a neighbour's, just to be safe?'

'Ooh, I couldn't leave him here on his own. Goodness knows what he might do. I've got some nice things, you know, and he could—'

Her voice continued indignantly as he ran out to the car. 'Emergency!' he shouted at the duty sergeant on the front desk. He would ring Mott while he drove. If this intruder was Roger Bascombe, who had been reported as having eluded the PC who'd been sent to bring him in at Maidenhead, he could be trying to track Jenny down; and, now that he was at Jamie's flat, perhaps he was hoping to do it the way Silver had – through the man's computer.

* * *

Accompanied by the senior medical registrar, Yeadings stared into the intensive care ward. A nurse had opened slats in the vertical blinds when Dr Cartright tapped on the window.

'Can't let you in, I'm afraid. Fear of infection, you know. But, due to the exceptional circumstances, your access to his records has been approved. You suspect the poisoning was deliberate?'

'There could have been a serious attempt to kill him.'

'Which may still succeed, I'm afraid. He should have seen his GP as soon as the symptoms appeared. He would be in agony by now, but for the morphine.'

Standing here watching the man slowly die would be pointless. He was past giving any information. Yeadings was reminded of the ghastly press photographs of the Russian refugee poisoned with Polonium. 'No chance, I suppose, that a radioactive substance was used on him?'

'No. He was thoroughly tested for that. The final diagnosis was antimony poisoning. You don't get a lot of that nowadays. Regulations are pretty stringent in metal processing. Of course, accidents can happen, as anywhere. You need, perhaps, to find out whether he was involved in any way with the manufacture of semiconductors. There may be risk to others like him. The Department of Public Health has been notified. They'll be working to trace the source.'

'And no indication of a history of drug abuse – heroin, cocaine, Ecstasy?'

'None. He wasn't a user. Apart from this he was a well-developed, fit fifty-nine-year-old.'

* * *

Mott's number was engaged. Beaumont punched out Athene's. She might be out or taking an early night, and he could be wasting his time. But she answered, bright and precise as ever. It didn't faze her that he was on his way. 'It'll be nice to see you,' she said briskly. 'I'll switch the kettle on.'

A second attempt to reach Mott was successful. Beaumont reported that he was hunting up Farlow's background, without actually naming Athene as his source.

'Well, don't be all night. We're thin on the ground at present. I sent Z home early with the start of a cold, and Silver's gone to bring Roger Bascombe in.'

Which leaves DI Salmon, Beaumont thought. So where was old Fishface?

'No panic, Angus. The Boss is still at his desk: captain of the ship, last to go down with it.'

He heard Angus's snort of appreciation as he cut the call.

Z had not gone home. Max wouldn't be there. He'd taken a couple of days off to check on a dubious charity working out of Plymouth. It might be worth a column or two.

She sucked a cough sweet in her car and decided her throat was less raspy. The present case – or cases? – had stalled. Among the crowd of characters they had had to interview, no obvious suspect had come forward either for the killer or the Telehouse drug dealer.

By now she was almost certain that Jenny had ended up in the torched Audi, her absence unaccounted for since this afternoon's message from Cumbrian police. They had traced Jamie to a cottage at Bassenthwaite, where he had happened on a local divorcee ten years his senior and settled in. No other female had been observed with him, and the couple claimed not to have heard the radio or television news.

Too busy, Z guessed. So Jenny hadn't gone fell-walking with him. But that didn't mean he hadn't disposed of her before he set out.

Blu-tacked to a wall of the tea bar at Telehouse, Z had earlier found a group photograph of techs being briefed by the floor manager. She had helped herself to it, to keep in mind their names and how they fitted into the operation. She slipped it out of her notebook now. Among the crowd was Nicco Facci, looking attentive; the lighting man, Winslow, sulky, as if just reprimanded; Jenny, appearing critical and hugging a laptop. Jamie was in profile, but his features were clear as he issued orders.

Would old Mr Rennie recognise him as a constant visitor at Jenny's?

She decided to go now and find out.

Chapter Twenty

Miss Shelby's hand trembled as she tried to replace the receiver. The strange man was at the bottom of the stairs and advancing on her, terrible anger in his eyes. A crumpled paper in his hand was shoved in his pocket as he reached for her bony wrist. She cried out at the sharp arthritic pains shooting through her.

'Who were you phoning?' he yelled, shaking her.

'My butcher,' she lied in desperation.

'At this time of night? I'll "butcher" you, you old bag. It was the police, wasn't it? Yes, I thought so.' He pushed her against the hall table and it went crashing over with her on top, spilling her precious knick-knacks.

She managed to roll onto her knees, foolishly grabbing at his trouser leg to help herself up. He shook her off roughly and made for the front door.

It seemed he'd got what he'd come for. She felt an enormous relief that she was to be rid of him without further assault, but ashamed at letting down the nice Mr Silver, who was already on his way to apprehend the horrid man. She ought to do something, *anything*, to delay him.

She reached with both hands for the Axminster runner that ran along the centre of the passage floor and pulled with all her puny, painful strength. Caught unaware with one foot lifted and a hand about to release the spring lock, he stumbled, catching his left temple on the wire basket of the letterbox. He cried out as blood spurted down his cheek, and kicked backwards, missing her, as he covered his face with his hands.

Miss Shelby crawled back in the direction of the kitchen. Huddled and trembling, she heard him let himself out. The door swung in the chill wind but she had no strength to go and shut it. He'd got away, but she had done her best to stop him. And, injured, he might not get far.

That wire basket, how providential that she'd had it installed. It had been a security measure recommended in a talk given at the Townswomen's Guild. You screwed it on the inner side of your front door to stop anyone putting nasty things through the letterbox which could catch fire or make a disgusting smell. The speaker had been right. There were some really unpleasant people about these days.

In his car, Roger Bascombe scrabbled through the glove compartment with one hand while blood poured down over the other. It mixed with the dribble from his nose. No tissues. He had to use a couple of old parking tickets to mop up because he couldn't drive with blood running in his eyes.

So now the police had an update on him, but he counted on their reaction being dilatory as ever, unless there was a patrol car already in this area. But he must get away at once. Every minute wasted kept him longer from satisfying his urgent need. Now that he had Jenny's address he must catch up with her, and any supplies she kept at home.

On the way to Notting Hill he just might happen on an all-night chemist's and get his forehead fixed with a strip of Band-Aid. It was galling to think that, open mainly to supply kids with their prescription drugs, they'd have the very stuff he needed on the premises.

When he saw the open front door Silver knew Roger had eluded them again. He was a slippery beggar, but he wouldn't get far. If he had found Jenny's address, was obvious where he'd be heading, and with luck could be beaten to it.

First there was Miss Shelby to look to. She hadn't appeared as his car squealed to a halt outside. He ran in, calling her name, and heard a feeble reply from the rear of the house. There were signs of a skirmish in the passage, with the floor rug rucked up and a small table overturned among smashed china. He stepped over it, opened the kitchen door and found the old lady cowering under the table.

She didn't appear seriously injured, but you couldn't tell what might have happened to her. In any case, she mustn't stay here overnight alone. He helped her into a chair and phoned for an ambulance. His second call was to DS Zyczynski's mobile. Briefly he explained what had happened and where Bascombe would be making for. 'Can you cover? Be careful, though. He's in a very excitable state and vicious. I'll follow up when I'm free here.'

* * *

Beaumont counted his way along the row of almost identical small, modern houses with white window frames and red roof tiles – or identical when first built. As a sure sign of owner occupation, extensions and adornments had been added to them all in various styles and with varying taste. Athene's aspirations to individuality were modest, being a tidy little wooden porch at the front door and a blue-painted trellis to either side of the downstairs windows, up which plants showed early intentions of climbing. He noted, too, a discreet burglar alarm.

Before he could ring, the door opened. Athene welcomed him with a friendly grin. There was little here of the cool professional he'd met at Telehouse. Her hair, no longer severely pulled back in an elastic band, was loose on her shoulders, slightly wavy; a shade between blonde and light brown, not unlike what he now appreciated was the colour of her eyes.

'Hello, you managed to find me,' she greeted him.

'Sat Nav,' he said drolly.

'I know, but it's a traditional question for a first visit.' This made him wonder if she expected him to call again. If so, professionally or for personal pleasure?

She waved him in. 'I remember reading a book once in which almost all the first chapter was taken up by a middle-aged couple arriving as guests of an older man and the three discussing the entire journey and their opinions on the best routes to make it.'

Beaumont grimaced, entering the lounge and succumbing to a cream leather chair under the window. 'Sounds quite boring. I'm surprised you remember it.'

'Actually it was fascinating. Nobody could agree. The nuances in their conversation were amazing. You got to know so much about them solely from the way they reacted to each other on such a mundane subject. I wish I could write like that.'

'You're pretty amazing at your own job, I'd say.'

'But it's a distraction from what I enjoy most.'

'Which is?'

'I write fiction. Not scripts, because in them too much depends on the actor's interpretation and the director's manipulation. No, it's the balance of narrative, dialogue and description that fascinates me.'

'Have you...?' Beaumont began, and then halted from fear of being tactless.

'...been published? Yes, my first two, on a three-book contract. I'm an eighth of the way through the third. They're doing well in America. That's how I came to buy this house. Not so well over here, though. We Brits do inertia publishing, no advertising to speak of and rare press reviews of living authors. Readers don't buy. They rely on a good library service.'

'You're impressive. I'll have to get one of your books.'

'Now don't boggle at me. Writers are like everyone else, just doing their job. I don't know why people think we're different. Mind, it's useful. Once they know what you do there's no limit to their helping out with information. They'll even pour their hearts out: things they've never confided to anyone else.'

She grinned again. 'Have you eaten?'

He confessed he hadn't, and lunch had been a sausage

roll snatched from the canteen and abandoned half-eaten when Mott had pulled him in on an interview.

'So what shall we have? Come through and choose.'

He followed her into the diminutive kitchen, marvelling how it felt that he'd always known her.

Mott's instruction to him on leaving had been a casual, 'Don't be all night.' He found himself hoping now that by some lucky turn of fate a stay-over might be on the cards.

DS Zyczynski pulled in to the kerb to take Silver's message about Roger Bascombe. 'I'm halfway there already,' she told him 'I'll check on Jenny's flat and then wait for him to arrive. If he looks dangerous, I'll contact the Met for back-up.'

'Do that anyway,' Silver advised.

Z smiled to herself. She didn't see the failing actor as any threat to her. Jamie's elderly aunt must have given a highly coloured version of his visit, probably fell over in the hall when she caught her foot in the rug. Silver was a real softy when it came to the old and infirm.

When she pulled into the road opposite the art framing shop, she saw lights showing on both floors. Someone was upstairs in Jenny's curtained flat, or else she had an automatic switching system in order to fool would-be burglars. If so, it was strange no one had remarked on it before. She was more than ready to accept Jenny's had been the body in the burnt-out car but, if so, who was up there in the flat? Had a customer broken in to raid her stock?

Z left the car and went across. There was a slightly

different arrangement in the window now: a large watercolour landscape having been replaced by a 3ft by 3ft canvas depicting Moscow's Red Square by moonlight. On the ground floor a narrow central gap in the black curtains behind the displayed pictures allowed a glimpse of the saleroom, but Duncan Rennie wasn't there. If she craned sideways she could make out the door to the staircase and some wrapped canvases in a heap holding it ajar. She decided to contact Rennie first. Then, until Bascombe turned up, she could wait below and cut off his retreat to make her arrest. She pressed the doorbell.

Inside the shop, nothing moved. She waited and tried again. Perhaps Rennie was working late, occupied with varnishing or framing in the rear of the premises. She would drive round to the back and hope to get in that way.

Confronted by the electronically controlled gate to his small timber yard, she gave up. Through its bars, she could make out more lights behind the downstairs windows, which appeared to be of pebbled glass.

There remained no alternative to risking entry into Jenny's flat and waiting for Bascombe there. High on whatever she'd supplied (and possible high-dosing), he'd made the marked improvement Margot had been working for in those final scenes, which had amazed the rest of the cast. And now, days later, with Jenny's disappearance, Roger had used up whatever she'd sold him then and, knowing of no other source, was half-crazed to get his next fix.

He could be a difficult prisoner to bring in. She could

have done with back-up and the long-refused warrant to search the premises. Two magistrates Yeadings had approached considered there to be insufficient proven evidence to risk breaching the woman's Civil Rights.

Z drove back to the front of the building, uncertain whether in the meantime Roger had arrived and gained access to the upper flat. None of the half dozen cars parked in the road looked familiar. She could be in time.

She took her flashlight from the car's glove compartment and approached the blue street door that led directly upstairs. Hesitating before ringing, she shone the torch over it and made out a distortion of the brass lock-face. The centre appeared to have been drilled out. She pushed the door gently and it opened halfway.

She slid into the square hall. On her left was the door leading into Duncan Rennie's shop, left ajar with the wrapped canvases leaning against it. She stepped through and called softly, 'Mr Rennie, are you there?'

There was no answer, no movement. It seemed likely that he had gone upstairs before going home, leaving his own lights on and accounting for the lights she had seen behind Jenny's curtains. He could have noticed damage to the street door and gone up to see if everything was all right in Jenny's flat. But he hadn't struck her as so absent-minded that he'd leave his own premises vulnerable.

Going up quietly, listening for sounds of movements, she felt the short hairs on her neck stiffen as she sensed something very wrong. Halfway up, she heard music playing. Either Jenny was alive and had returned or someone else was making himself at home. There were crashing chords against the constant jungle thrumming of the base, and then a strangled, androgynous voice started up, shouting the words.

It wasn't part of the recording; more like some drunken Saturday-night karaoke performance in a pub. Whoever was up there was well away, whether on alcohol or something to snort. It seemed possible Roger Bascombe had got in while she checked at the rear, and he'd made a big hit on Jenny's stash.

But, in that case, what had happened to Duncan Rennie from downstairs?

Z opened her mobile, uncertain whom to call. Yeadings' team was spread about the three counties and, as Mott kept saying, they were thin on the ground for such a rush of major crime as the last two weeks had provided.

She decided to go for uniform and rang Control at Maidenhead, identified herself and demanded an emergency shout, giving her location, the situation, and warning she was about to go in.

'Not alone,' the sergeant warned. 'Z, you have to wait for back-up. I'll notify the Met. Just wait till they can get someone to you.'

But already it was too late. In a pause in the music her voice had alerted the reveller inside the flat. The door opened abruptly, dazzling her with multicoloured points of light, and against them, the grotesque figure of a tall woman silhouetted in a see-through evening gown.

Chapter Twenty-One

It was late, but before leaving for home Superintendent Yeadings walked into the analysis room and studied the collection of photographs on the extended whiteboard running the length of one wall. The office manager was still there, looking worried. Anyone could appreciate there was too much information on hand, too many people under examination. Some revelation was needed to eliminate a large number, but as yet it was impossible to recognise a clear direction leading towards the prime mover behind the criminal events.

In any organisation made up of strong personalities with complex functions, small scandals and petty crimes would inevitably be uncovered once one started to scratch at the surface. Like anywhere else, there was in-house politicking. Jealousies arose from frustrated ambition; and pressures exercised by natural manipulators preyed on weaker minds. God knows, it was the same in the police.

He paused at the still shots of Oliver Charrington's body on the floor of the set. They had been shifted to one corner, awaiting the result of the resumed coroner's inquest in five days' time. Below them were Blu-tacked sheets recording the final messages received on his wife's mobile phone, which could have pushed him to take his own life, and the medical report from Dr Frobisher. Unless something untoward turned up in the meantime, it seemed that the verdict would more likely be suicide than accidental death.

Now, in central position and dated two days later, were photographs of the burnt-out Audi Cabriolet with the obscene contents of its boot and Prof Littlejohn's findings on examination of the female body. Margot Charrington's name underneath had been crossed through and another substituted: Jenny Barnes, followed by a question mark.

It was Mott who had added that last, but Yeadings was convinced that the query should be removed. And if Jenny had been the drugs dealer, which Roger Bascombe's desperate behaviour now seemed to imply, was it credible that he had been the one to strangle her after some altercation and, in so doing, cut off his own supply? Not intentionally, unless he had a more direct source to tap, which, clearly, he hadn't. But if she was withholding supplies he could still be the killer, overcome by rage and underestimating his own strength.

But who else had Jenny been supplying? A team of DCs augmented by constables seconded from the uniform division had been beavering away at fresh interviews of everyone involved in the production of *All Fired Up*, examining the technicians' CVs and in-house annual assessments, dredging for gossip about personal scandals. But the core of the trouble could still be someone outside their number. The ever-haunting shadow of Character X could, by accident or design, have been behind the torched car and its as yet unidentified body. Except that it had been stolen from a security area at the studios. So this swung the pointer back to Telehouse personnel.

Other television programmes were safely reaching the screen without incurring such real life tragedies as Oliver's death, the murdered woman in the torched Audi, and the poisoning of a middle-aged lighting expert, news of whose death was expected at any moment. Must he consider accident and natural causes anywhere in these events, or had there been a single mind controlling a sequence?

Starting at the top with the producer, Greg Victor: how would he shape up for the part? As far as Yeadings could see, he was an ideas man whose line was to retire from the scene of action once he'd flung a cat among the pigeons. Next in seniority stood Margot, but she had come off badly as a result of all that had happened. It was inconceivable that such a skilled organiser could have manoeuvred herself into such a wretched situation. Not that her sudden widowing had exactly shattered her, but she'd lost face badly with the team she directed. News of her manipulation by young Niccolo Facci, with an agenda mainly on the sexual level, would be relished by those she worked with. She was furious and shamed by her own submission to him, but their involvement with each other had simplified the investigation, supplying them both with alibis for the car's torching and the woman's (surely Jenny's) death.

So, Jenny, Margot's assistant director and red-haired biker: what a complex character she was turning out to

267

be. The demanding studio job hadn't been enough for her. The quantity of drugs found there must surely imply she'd been lucratively supplying a ring of users, although as yet there was no compelling forensic evidence to back this up. But, while holding some strong cards, she must surely have come off worse than anyone.

Roger Bascombe, failing actor and possibly hooked on a habit, was a weak character who covered inadequacy with bluster, lost his nerve under pressure and did daft things. He could have started a sequence of accidents, but hardly had the drive or intelligence to be behind everything that went wrong from Friday night onwards. More and more it appeared that in an outburst of befuddled frustration he had killed Jenny, and in what looked at first like a desperate search for her was merely a need to get to her supplies.

On that Friday night, if Roger had killed Jenny at the end of the shoot, hadn't Margot's disappearance with Nicco been a godsend? Able to take her car to transport Jenny's body to a country lane, he would have hidden it in woodland until the next night and then burnt all the evidence.

Yeadings mused aloud on this and the office manager came across to join him. 'In which case he'd be the one on Jenny Barnes's bike who picked up the can of petrol on the Saturday night.'

That scenario was surely too complex. It would imply an enormous amount of organisation and Yeadings wasn't persuaded that Roger had been capable of that, especially in his dependent state. How many extra visits could he have made to Telehouse to recover his own car and Jenny's Kawasaki without arousing security's suspicion?

He voiced his doubts.

'Unless by Saturday he took a friend along to help out.'

Yeadings considered this. He couldn't see Roger having that kind of friend. The man was self-contained, competitive, spiky, almost a loner.

He abandoned all thought of Bascombe as the killer, but the word *loner* hung on in his head, like something half-remembered that wouldn't let up on him. Of course, a loner was what he was looking for – someone who did everything for himself, through himself. There were robust egos aplenty among the crowd at Telehouse, but the interactive nature of their work and an ingrained studio culture produced an appearance of companionship. Some could be genuinely congenial; others putting on an act.

He needed to know much more about the persons behind these photographs. Maybe he'd find what he needed in the CVs his augmented team had been working through. Within the listed groups there would certainly have been minor irritants which could work towards major events. Bascombe would not have been the only user dependent on Jenny. Once they caught up with him, he should be able to suggest other names to consider as suspects for the killing.

And where exactly was Bascombe now? DC Silver's most recent message to Control had located him on his way by road to Jenny Barnes's flat in Notting Hill, with Zyczynski in close pursuit. She might even have been in time to cut him off, but she hadn't reported back since that emergency call for back-up. Silver, following her, had more ground to cover, and for a period she would be on her own. The Met had been notified. It was up to them, and dependent on current pressures, how seriously they ranked the need. For himself, he was concerned for her safety.

All he could do now was await developments. Going home was out of the question with such a feeling in his gut of something critically in the balance. He was tempted to ring Z direct, but she might be at some vital point in the arrest. Instead, he rang home and told Nan he'd not be back until morning. She took it as calmly as ever, said there was plenty in the fridge for when he did make it, and the children were asleep in bed. She thought she might toddle off there herself.

Yeadings went down to the deserted senior mess. He could hear whistling from the kitchen and went through. A man in starched whites was squirting disinfectant over the surfaces and cheerfully waved a tea towel at him. 'You still here, sir? Feeling a bit peckish?'

'I wondered if there was anything left...'

'Got a nice bit of Scottish steak, sir. Give me twenty minutes and I'll rustle up as good a meal as the real chef does.'

'Twenty it is then. Medium rare, thank you.'

He returned to his office, tidied his desktop, checked the BBC News Channel and looked reproachfully at the pair of silent phones. When he returned to the mess the orderly proudly presented a piled plate of steak and onions, towering crinkle chips, broccoli and carrots, with lashings of horseradish on the side. There was a half bottle of Jacob's

Creek Shiraz Cabernet to chase it down.

On a restricted-carbohydrate diet, Yeadings imagined what comment Nan would have made about portion control.

'This,' he told the orderly, 'is what I'd call a Policeman's Lot.'

Halfway through the meal his phone rang. It was Wycombe Hospital. Barry Farlow had died half an hour ago. A post-mortem was scheduled for the next day at 3.15.

Another suspicious death with no clear reason or motive. And a further possible link with the drugs business?

Yeadings laid down his fork and pushed his plate away.

DC Silver drew into the kerb ten yards short of Z's Toyota. Any of the cars parked at various points in the road could be Bascombe's. He hadn't picked up details on it before setting out and he didn't want a query to delay him now. It was fifty-fifty whether the man had arrived already.

He noted lights behind the curtained windows of Jenny's flat. A street lamp threw an orange glow over the window of the arty old chap's shop, and when he went close he could see the lit interior through a thin chink in the blackout behind the pictures on display.

He decided to alert old Rennie to possible trouble upstairs, located a bell-push high at the side of the entrance and gave it three short jabs.

There was no movement inside even when he rang again. He applied gentle pressure to the door, but it was securely locked. He moved on to the blue street door that led up to the flat and saw it stood slightly ajar. The Chubb lock's centre had been drilled out.

This didn't look good. He could have done with a couple of hefties from uniform with their Tasers at the ready. He went back to the car for his magnum flashlight. If there was to be trouble inside, at least he had a weapon.

On the staircase, he listened before going up. Loud, throbbing music was coming from the flat; which should have been reassuring but wasn't. Too often, he knew from similar situations, it could be used to cover more brutal noises. He crept close, hefted the flashlight and pressed gently on the door panels.

He found himself in a small, square hall. Four doors stood wide open, showing rooms lit with multicoloured spotlights. The music was coming from ahead. That would be the large room overlooking the road. He edged towards it, glancing as he passed into a tiny kitchen, narrow bathroom and a room almost entirely filled by a double bed covered by psychedelic-coloured fabrics. Sprawled on it was someone partly obscured by a tall, gaunt woman bending over. She was tense, exerting pressure on the recumbent body.

Silver lunged forward and grabbed her by the waist, meaning to force her down and whip her wrists back for cuffing. But he hadn't brought cuffs. And there was no one to provide them.

The woman seized his instant of hesitation, twisted to face him and landed a crashing blow to his chin. He went down, but she grasped a handful of his anorak to pull him up and landed another and another to his belly. All his breath went out. He doubled up. Over the shattering pain he could just register her arm raised with some heavy object and then it came crashing down on his skull.

As Silver slowly emerged from the mental fog, he lay trying to remember how he came to be there. He felt across the surface of jumbled garments and encountered a body. Heaving himself onto an elbow he peered at it.

Never in his wildest dreams had he expected to share a bed with Rosemary Zyczynski.

His pockets had been emptied. He ran his hands over the DS in search of her radio, but hers, too, was gone.

The strange woman – he paused, uncertain. *Was* she a woman? Tall and lanky, she'd packed a punch worthy of a navvy. The clothes had deceived him. He tried to remember how she looked in that brief moment when he'd grabbed her and she spun to face him. The body had been hard. Under her red hair the features had been heavily made up, with streaky, ill-applied mascara, so that she gave the impression of having recently wept. In a way, she'd slightly resembled Jenny Barnes, as if they could be related. And she'd been dressed for a party or a formal dinner.

No, he decided: she was a man. It was too shaming to have been knocked out by a woman.

Z remained unconscious, white-faced with blood congealing on one temple and having pooled over the pillow. The man had done this, struck her with some kind of weapon. Perhaps the same he'd used on Silver later. And he'd carried Z in here and laid her out on the bed. Why? To care for her after what he'd done – or to strangle and rape her?

Silver tried to sit up and suppressed a groan. It could be he'd arrived in time to prevent something worse happening. But where was the man now? The music had stopped and the whole flat lay silent.

The main priority was Z. He was reassured to find a faint but regular pulse below her ear, but she couldn't be left without medical treatment. He must find some way to disable the attacker and raise an alarm. But he'd dropped his torch as he reached out to pinion the woman and couldn't see it on the floor.

Where the hell was the old man from downstairs? Hadn't he come up here? For an instant he'd believed the man dressed in women's clothes was Rennie. He was tall and skinny enough, but he could never pack a punch like that at his age. So perhaps he'd gone home as usual, and their attacker was the one who'd disarranged things downstairs and left the lights on. But there would be a phone in the shop. He needed only to get out of the flat unseen and go to summon help.

Gently, he rolled Z into the recovery position, unsure whether with a head injury she wouldn't be better left on her back. He'd never done much First Aid, relying too much on his value as a computer expert. When he got out of this – if he got out of this – he'd give some thought to taking a course in A & E.

He left the bed and went to listen at the door. There came a sound of crockery being shifted in the kitchen. Was the man getting himself a meal? That could distract him enough to overlook his prisoners.

There came a sudden crash of dishes hitting the floor

and smashing. 'Fuck, fuck, fuck!' the man shouted. Then more smashing.

Silver had to pass by the door. He glimpsed the wild sweep of the man's arm as he cleared the last objects from the cupboard's shelves. He was acting crazy. The floor was covered in debris that must have been there even before Silver had arrived.

The DC had attended scenes like this. The man wasn't just trashing the premises. He was desperately searching for something. So, assuming Jenny had been the Telehouse drug supplier, had he, like Bascombe, expected to find her main stash here?

In a brief respite from the smashes, Silver heard Z groan. Her attacker heard it too and spun on his heels, saw Silver and lunged towards him.

Oh God, not again, Silver thought as, groggily, he tried to avoid the blows. Like an unstrung puppet he was lifted and shaken, dropped on a kitchen chair and slumped there, helpless, while the man-woman ran out. But not letting him go free. He was back at once with an armful of the clothes that had littered the bed, dropped them on the floor and began to tie Silver down with what looked like a shimmering green evening gown.

He left and came back with Z struggling weakly in his arms. So much for Thames Valley's finest, Silver thought. We're not up to much, getting taken like this. How long, dear lord, before the cavalry arrives?

He wasn't certain he'd put a message through to Control. The first blow to his head seemed to have knocked his brains out of action. And even if he had got through, it would take an age for back-up to reach them from Thames Valley. By now, CID would all have gone home, unless the Boss was on one of his marathon prowls. Control would have to contact the Met and hope a local patrol car heeded their need.

Z had been dropped on a chair alongside and was being tied to it with something patterned. He saw that without it she would have toppled off.

'Call an ambulance,' Silver croaked. 'She's in a bad way.'

The tall person snarled something in reply and came across with a scarf to gag him. He was busy with it when the doorbell shrilled.

It startled them all. 'Up here,' Silver tried to bellow, but harsh material was thrust into his mouth and only a gurgle emerged.

Chapter Twenty-Two

Superintendent Yeadings sat bolt upright, the CV printout in one hand. This could be it.

For once he needed to resort to the computer because events were at a critical, even dangerous, stage. Not quite a Luddite, he had greater confidence in signed and dated paperwork than the product of pecking at an electronic keyboard. Nevertheless, under pressure and in view of the limited expanse of even his oversize desk, he intended seeking correlation via the risky route of IT incompetence.

He logged on, selected the Telehouse folder and entered the file listed as Interviews. The name he sought was near the end, but the information given was of no help at all.

Where else should he go? Bring up the interview with Athene, the all-seeing, all-knowing, of course. But those notes also were short of what he was looking for. Yet there was something he'd seen, seen or heard, days back in the investigation, which was nudging at his memory; so where was it?

He cleared the screen and keyed in Mott's scrupulous notes on each development in the case. This was modelled on his own age-old habit of keeping a handwritten diary which recorded, moment by moment, every event, every impression and every suspicion considered, whether followed up or abandoned. The loft at home was filled with cartons of minute observations collected since he first made DI sixteen years ago. Nan teased that they could form the future basis for a twelve volume autobiography. His excuse in response had been that he couldn't see the way ahead unless he was very sure of exactly where he stood at the time. 'It fixes me,' he'd explained. 'It's just the way my mind needs to work.' And it had paid dividends over the years.

He clicked on Edit and Find, feeding in his suspect's name selected from the pile of CVs. Still no record of the confirmation he was seeking. Yet this disturbing half-memory still hung in the air: someone's voice here in his office throwing it out casually and nobody picking up on it. An unconsidered quote from Athene, but he needed confirmation of the name.

He glanced down at the time. She'd most likely be in bed asleep, but he had to know right now. He brought up her landline number and asked the switchboard to put him through.

The call was answered after five rings by a familiar voice. He suppressed a demand why his DS was there.

'It's Yeadings,' he said shortly.

'Boss, what's up?'

'I need a word with Athene.'

'She's in the shower. I'll give her a call.'

Yeadings had a quickly suppressed vision of a naked

Beaumont recumbent among tangled sheets. He hadn't foreseen anything like this. It could have prejudiced the DS's part in the case; maybe even raised a disciplinary charge.

Athene sounded concerned. 'Has something happened?'

He explained while she rubbed her hair dry on a towel. 'Yes,' she told him. 'You're right. It was just after Margot gave up in despair and told Jenny to take Roger off and sort him out. She had a few words with him, disappeared for three or four minutes behind the cyc and then took him into the Gents for a private parley.'

'She slipped away long enough to pick up some cocaine for his fix?'

'I guess so, but that latter part I never saw.'

'And you are quite clear about who it was you saw follow her behind the cyc when she went for the stuff?'

'Yes.' She confirmed the name.

'Thank you, Athene. You've been a great help.' So now he knew. He had the name of the double killer. He hoped fervently that the man hadn't already added to the score.

Roger Bascombe moved backwards on the pavement and glared up at the lit windows. He watched a shadow pass behind a curtain, leant forward and kept his finger on the bell. Jenny might have good reason to fear after-dark visitors, but she had to get it into her head that his need was urgent, paramount.

He'd never felt as sick as this before. It was her fault; the high dose and then being cut off completely. He hadn't been using for more than a few weeks, so you couldn't

279

say he was hooked; no, not really. He wouldn't be in such a state now if she hadn't sent him on a high, under pressure to get that final scene shot for Margot. She'd a lot to answer for. If she tried to hold out on him now she'd damn well find out he wasn't the sucker she'd played him for. She was bloody incompetent as a supplier and mainly to blame for his being written out of the series. It all came back to Jenny. The longer she kept him waiting out here in the cold, the more his anger against her surged.

Still with one finger on the bell, he hammered with a fist on the door. And it gave way. He stumbled into an unlit hall with a straight staircase rising dimly ahead of him.

The house was silent as the grave. His hands ran over the walls to either side, found a light switch, but it was ineffective. Not that that was going to hold him back. He felt his way up, saw a wedge of light spilling onto a square landing, and pushed on ahead, into what must be the girl's apartment.

She came forward to meet him, looking unusually tall in a full-length gown. He bunched his fists, ready to meet opposition. 'Jenny!' he snarled. It stopped her in her tracks.

'Jenny,' she repeated in a trance-like whisper.

And then he saw that she wasn't; wasn't Jenny at all, but someone older, bigger, yet in some way similar, with the same red hair.

He started at a loud crash in the room she'd come out of. Silver, rocking on the kitchen chair, had managed to overbalance, landing painfully on one shoulder. He

280

grunted throatily into his gag, uncertain who'd just arrived, but knowing it wasn't police reinforcements: the approach was too amateur.

'You're *not* Jenny!' Bascombe accused, advancing on her. 'Who are you, and where the devil is she?'

'Jenny's...dead,' a girl's voice called faintly from the room ahead. 'He...killed...her.'

'*No!*' It was a high-pitched scream. 'I – am – Jenny. Sweet Jenny Barnes. I am! I am!'

'Call...999,' the unseen woman pleaded.

Bascombe stood open-mouthed, while in the kitchen the phone rang and went on ringing unanswered. Out in the street, a loud hailer sounded over the clatter of an approaching helicopter dropping low over the rooftops. A dazzling light swung across the windows.

The tall woman moaned, covering her face with her hands. She staggered and appeared to shrink as Bascombe watched, loose sleeves falling back to reveal muscled arms. He saw then that she wasn't a proper woman, but a lanky man in drag, a man he'd seen before, almost every day that he'd worked on the *All Fired Up* series.

'Come out unarmed with your hands on your head,' commanded the amplified voice from the helicopter.

No one moved. 'Help...us,' the unseen woman begged.

Bascombe pushed past the false Jenny, who had collapsed against the wall, and went into the kitchen, saw Silver, tied to a chair, sprawled on the floor. He recognised Zyczynski as the young female detective who'd interviewed them after Oliver Charrington fell from the grid. She was struggling feebly to get free of some material that was

281

tightly binding her to another chair. He was aware of the false Jenny coming up behind, swung round, and put all the anger he'd stored against the real one into a single punch. The man went down and dissolved into tears, his head between his knees, sobbing Jenny's name over and over again.

Roger nursed his sore knuckles. There was a case of kitchen knives on the wall over the working surface. He reached for a carver and started to saw through Silver's bonds.

'Welcome…the cavalry,' the DC croaked as the gag was removed and he struggled to his feet.

In a daze, his unlikely rescuer realised he'd finally played the hero and stood back for recognition. But, as boots pounded up the stairs, Silver shook him by the arm. 'What's his name again?'

'Who?'

'That.' Pointing at the man in drag.

'Winslow. Carl Winslow. He's assistant to the lighting gaffer.'

Silver put a hand on the mock Jenny's shoulder, made the arrest and recited the official caution. He completed the arrest as a number of uniforms from the Met crowded into the room.

'My prisoner,' he claimed, 'but thanks for almost being in time. I need to borrow a set of cuffs. And will someone undo my DS and summon an ambulance?'

The local men had contested the arrest, because the hostage taking had occurred on their patch. But a charge of double murder had priority, backed up forcibly by Mott when the Chiltern Chopper, commandeered by Yeadings, had contrived to find landing space and the DCI was rushed to the scene. He pointed out that there was an opportunity here for some special cooperation between the two Forces following a splendid bit of back-up.

It wasn't until daylight that the Met's SOCO team penetrated the lower reaches of the building and found Duncan Rennie's body in the little timber yard behind it.

'Defenestration,' their police surgeon pompously announced. To Yeadings, it appeared a phantom echo of Charrington's fall, which had started the web of events at Maidenhead. But this death was neither suicide nor accident. The elderly man had injuries arising from a frenzied attack. Disoriented by his sudden arrival, Winslow had beaten him up and disposed of his body through a rear window.

While Thames Valley prepared to charge Carl Winslow with the double murder of Jenny Barnes and his one-time boss, Barry Farlow, Scotland Yard began to build a similar scenario for the death of Duncan Rennie.

'Not,' Yeadings explained to his team at the final debriefing, 'that he's likely to stand trial on any of the charges. He'll be found unfit to plead. Now that a neighbour of Duncan Rennie's has identified him as a man observed on several occasions hanging about the road and watching the premises, it's certain that for some time he had been stalking Jenny Barnes.

'While your final drama was building up in Notting

Hill, I noticed almost a year was missing from his CV applying for the job at Maidenhead, and enquiries now reveal he was sectioned under the Mental Health Act and held in a psychiatric hospital in the West Midlands. Under medication, his condition improved. He was released and trained as an electrician. That is when he applied to Telehouse and was taken on as a lighting technician.

'His academic qualifications were above average. Earlier he'd dropped out of a BSc course at Brunel University "for health reasons", after he'd run amok with a knife, wounding three fellow students.

'His second-year sandwich course had included placement with a firm in Reading which manufactures, among other things, semiconductors, in which the poison antimony is used. I have learnt only today that he was in the habit of returning there to look up former acquaintances: the only people, incidentally, that he ever attempted to socialise with. Those were the occasions when he could have acquired a supply of antimony.

'In a discussion I've had with Dr Frobisher, whom the Defence team have called as their expert witness to back a plea of mental incapacity, he confirms my opinion that Winslow had been quietly working up to his present state for months. Fixated on his perfect Jenny, he was secretly planning a glorious but totally unrealistic future with her which was then suddenly shattered by his discovery of the criminal sideline she was running at Telehouse.

'He admits habitually stalking her and that he followed when she went behind the cyc to pick up a small package from an unused circuit box and took Roger for a private talk. This was followed by the failing actor's sudden new confidence in tackling the revised scenes Greg had introduced.

'Familiar with the effects of rapid-action drugs, Winslow understood what was going on, and was determined to tackle Jenny about this. He followed her to the car park, but beyond that point he cannot recall what happened. He seems to have reinvented their relationship since then, sometimes seeking the lost love of his life and then trying to replace her.

'Frobisher believes, and I think we must agree with him, that Jenny had turned on Winslow with contempt. She didn't care what he thought of her: she was her own woman. He couldn't take this. He reached out for her, shook her by the throat and was left holding her lifeless body.

'He must have still had a tight enough grasp of reality over the next day to plan the disposal of the body and of the car he'd driven her off in, but he could not accept that Jenny was dead. From then on, he was in denial. The body's destruction had helped to remove that part of the truth for him. But there was a horrendous gap left. His life had no centre. He forgot to take his medication and, seeking her, he broke into her home, surrounded himself with her possessions. They all reassured him she was still alive to enjoy them; that she would soon walk through the door and be claimed by him.

'He grew to feel he belonged there in her home and the final slide into dementia came as he put on her make-up, dressed in her clothes, saw himself in her mirror. Jenny had returned. Life had some meaning for him again.

'And then his euphoria was threatened by strangers coming to his door, denying all he had achieved. How else could it have ended but in violence?'

'And the antimony poisoning,' Mott picked up. 'Quite when he conceived the idea of eliminating his boss isn't clear. We know he had access to the poison. There was more of it at his home. It would have been a deliberate and early detail in his strategy to replace Farlow and win Jenny. But that was always beyond reality. For her he didn't exist. On that Friday night in the car park, when he confronted her about the drugs, he couldn't take her scorn. Total rejection. We all know what savage retaliation that can excite.'

Beaumont was bristling in his seat. 'But at the time of stealing Margot's Audi and torching it with Jenny's body inside, he must have known what he was doing. Wasn't that motivated by a vicious mind? Or was he conveniently overtaken by a mental storm that saves him from accounting for his actions?'

Yeadings sighed, collecting his papers to show the debriefing was over. 'It's not for us to decide on his ability to stand trial. But in any case, he will be accounting for everything, locked in a secure place, for the rest of his life. Ironically, he'll be ever increasingly aware of what he has done if medication returns him to some kind of sanity.

'On the other hand, he may mercifully escape full realisation of his actions, and rigidly continue to believe he's become the girl he built his life around.'

'There's a lighter side to the story,' Mott rounded up as

they prepared to move off. 'Have you all seen the tabloids this morning? They're still not complimentary to Thames Valley Force, but Roger Bascombe's there on a wave of heroism, rescuing two of our officers held hostage by a triple murderer. *The Sun*'s running a half-page biog, plus pictures, on his rise to become one of our country's most distinguished comedy actors.'

The corners of DI Salmon's mouth turned further down. 'It'll not be long before he reappears on TV as a celebrity in one of those appalling "reality" shows. Let's hope he completes his rehab before then.'